MAYA NICOLE

DESCEND

CELESTIAL ACADEMY BOOK 2

Emily,
Just dream...
♡ Maya Nicole

Social Media

Be sure to join my Facebook group or signup for my newsletter for book release updates and sneak peaks!
https://www.facebook.com/groups/mayanicoleauthor/

Newsletter
https://mailchi.mp/2441120a2b47/mayanicole

Instagram @mayanicoleauthor

Twitter @MayaAuthor

Other Books by Maya Nicole

Celestial Academy

Ascend

Descend

Transcend

Playlist

Lover - Taylor Swift
Muddy Waters - LP
ADHD - Joyner Lucas
Come Back For Me - Jaymes Young
Life Support - Sam Smith
Million Eyes - Loïc Nottet
Creep - Radiohead
With or Without You - U2
Power - Isak Danielson
Oblivion - Bastille
Take What You Want - Post Malone ft. Ozzy
Osbourne, Travis Scott
Bitter End - Rag'n'Bone Man

Author's Note

Descend is a reverse harem romance. That means the main character will have a happily ever after with three or more men. This book also contains male/male romantic encounters, as well as several romantic encounters together as a group.

Some scenes may trigger some readers due to PTSD flashbacks, abduction, bullying, and a relationship with a teacher in a college academy setting.

Recommended for readers 18+ for adult content and language.

Prologue

Lucifer

18 Years Ago

I stood next to the gaping hole in the ground, the mahogany casket staring back at me. It was an inanimate object, but somehow I felt it was mocking me for opening my heart.

Opening my heart only to have it shattered to pieces.

The casket was the color of her hair; rich brown with a million other shades woven intricately in the strands. It was the reason I chose it.

I had walked into the funeral home with a pearlescent white casket in mind, but when I spotted the glistening mahogany, I knew it was the one.

I never thought instead of picking out an engagement ring, I'd be picking out a casket. I had the engagement all planned out. I would fill her coffee shop with a thousand lilies.

It didn't escape me now that lilies were also a funeral flower. The florist informed me they represented innocence being restored to the soul. Everyone ordered lilies for funerals.

Was that fact supposed to bring me peace?

It didn't.

I ordered them because they were her favorite flower. They were her namesake, Lily. Several wreaths of them lay atop the closed casket.

I stared at them, willing for this to be a twisted nightmare I was stuck in. It wouldn't be the first time I was stuck in a nightmare.

My whole existence had been one.

I looked to my left, and several feet away, stood John Adamson with his pregnant wife. She was due any day now. The two women had bonded over pregnancy stories and the excitement bringing a baby into the world brought.

I had wanted to kill John when he came into the waiting room, covered in blood, to tell me she was gone.

My Lily. Gone.

In that moment, it had taken every ounce of my being not to rip his throat out. I had wanted to be in the operating room, just in case.

I could have healed her.

He had said there was nothing to worry about. That the baby was showing no signs of having wings in the womb. That she was just a healthy baby girl and the birth would be standard.

A standard pregnancy. A standard birth. And it was, until it wasn't.

The umbilical cord was wrapped around her neck. She was in distress. Cesarean section or she would die. He told me to let him do his job.

Now Lily lay dead in a casket. She didn't even get to hold our daughter.

My chest tightened and my eyes burned with unshed tears. I wasn't a crier. At least until five days ago.

I brought the sleeping bundle in my arms closer to my body. She was a quiet newborn. She only cried when I cried. Somehow, I think she knew.

"Sir? Are you ready?"

My eyes snapped to the priest who looked at me with concern and pity. I was too tired and broken to care how he looked at me.

I nodded. I wasn't ready.

He pressed a button and the casket began to lower into the ground, taking my heart with it. I had given her my heart completely.

I was a fool for believing I'd ever find happiness.

My daughter made a small noise and I looked away from the scene in front of me and down at her tiny face. She had Lily's nose.

How was I going to do this? Raise a baby, alone, without Lily?

Her eyes opened for a moment and then shut, her tiny fists coming up near her chin and a smile forming on her face. My own lips twitched as I looked down at her.

I felt someone next to me and looked to find John and his wife. The small service was over. I had wanted to be alone for this, but John had convinced me to let them attend.

"Have you decided on a name for her yet?" He reached over and touched her little fist.

She would be a fighter, I could tell. She would have to be.

I looked back down at her, her mouth still curved in a smile as she slept. She was my world now. The one I would fight for, give my heart to, bleed for. Without her light, I would be lost in darkness.

"Her name is Danica."

Chapter One

Danica

I sat straight up, my heart pounding, my mind not quite sure where I was. I sprung from the bed, my legs getting twisted in my sheets. The floor met my face and a sharp pain went through my nose.

"Fuck!" I rolled over onto my back and pounded my fists on the floor. I stared at the ceiling, wondering if the nightmares would ever end.

My nose felt like it had been hit by a soccer ball and I brought my hand up to rub it. Luckily, it didn't bleed from its intimate acquaintance with the hardwood floor.

My nightmares seemed to be getting worse as the days went on. My only reprieve from them was on the weekends when I was with Asher.

On Sunday nights they would start and be

manageable, but by Thursday, they were enough to make me want to bash my head against the wall. Now they were, apparently, enough to almost break my nose.

Oliver's comfort superpower didn't help. Tobias just worried too much with his never-ending questions. The only comfort from the nightly terrors was to sleep at Asher's house. It was like when I was near him, my body knew he was safe and not lost forever.

It had been three weeks since Olly and Tobias returned with a newly unfallen Asher. Three weeks since they told me I was part of a cryptic prophecy delivered by a psychic. Three weeks since finding out my mother was possibly *the* Lilith.

"Your mom is Lilith."

The name played over and over in my head. What was I supposed to do with *that*?

I felt like I was on an episode of some prank show where at any moment a camera crew would jump out and scream "gotcha!" It had to be a sick, twisted joke.

I wasn't well versed in the Bible or even stories surrounding the Bible. But what I did know from television and fiction was that Lilith was not one of the good guys. There had to be a reason for that.

I held hope that it was all wrong. What I thought I knew about angels was certainly all wrong.

As soon as I had been alone after her name was

uttered, I had done the worst thing possible. I had internet searched the hell out of her. It was very similar to looking up medical symptoms. One minute it was just a name, and the next it was like a flesh-eating amoeba was gnawing at my insides and I only had three minutes to live.

There were so many stories about Lilith and none of them left me with a warm fuzzy feeling.

To add insult to injury, it was highly probable that the mysterious woman behind the angel abductions was *her*. John Adamson was involved. It couldn't purely be coincidence that the doctor who birthed me just happened to also be involved in an elaborate scheme to steal angel blood to open a gate to hell.

Everything had returned to normal. Most of the abducted angels that hadn't been part of the rescue operation were in heaven, healing mentally from their torture. Angels might not be able to die, but draining their blood day after day did a number on them.

Olly and I were back to school, Tobias resumed teaching his classes, and Asher continued to run his business.

Their guardian duties? *Me.*

Everything *seemed* normal, but it wasn't. I was freaking out.

I sat up from my place on the floor and glanced at the clock. It was only six. I had barely fallen asleep at two. I was exhausted and knew trying to sleep for another hour would be pointless.

I trudged to the bathroom and turned on the shower before peeling my damp pajamas off. I felt like I had run a marathon in my sleep, and looking in the mirror, I looked like it too.

Today was the last day before Spring break and most angels had guardian assignments to protect drunken college students partying it up in exotic locations. Warm waters and sandy beaches sounded like just the reprieve I needed.

I wasn't invited to the party because I wasn't an angel.

I showered quickly and attempted to cover up the dark circles under my eyes. They had progressively gotten worse throughout the week. I didn't need Tobias or Olly hovering over me because I looked like hell.

I had Spring break plans of my own and didn't need them worrying about me.

I dressed in my uniform and sat at my desk, opening my laptop. Most of my morning had become ritualistic lately. I would wake from a nightmare, shower and get dressed, then research Lilith and John Adamson.

I needed to know more about Lilith. It had become an addiction and scenarios ran through my brain constantly throughout the day. Someone had answers and that someone was John Adamson.

So, like any completely rational person, I

decided to go to the man who had overseen my birth. The same man who was behind draining angels of their blood. Completely a good idea, if I do say so myself.

I pulled up my password protected folder and opened a screenshot of the party invitation Ava sent me.

Every year, John Junior had a Spring break kick-off party. It was the party of the year, and even though I was still pissed as hell about what had gone down between us, I was going. I had a mission to accomplish, and since John Senior was seldom around, it would be easy to accomplish.

At least I hoped so.

The movies always made it look like a piece of cake to break into an office. If nothing else, I would snoop to try to figure out why John Senior would involve himself in such nefarious activities.

I closed the image of the party invitation and opened a document containing my mother's obituary. From what little my dad had told me growing up, she had no family. I thought nothing of it before, but now those little details raised red flags.

Lily Judith Gardener, age 25, passed away quietly on January 20, 2001. She was born April 30, 1975. She owned and operated Viva La Vida Coffee, a Montecito award winning coffee establishment. Lily was strong in spirit and brought light into the lives of those she met. She is survived by her life partner and newborn daughter.

I had read it at least a million times, and each

time my heart ached at the words "life partner." She had been my father's life. Had everything been a lie?

The obituary was short and simple, which was Lucifer's style. It didn't give me much information, other than she was not very creative with her name if she really was Lilith.

I had scoured the internet for her, but besides the coffee shop, there were no traces of her. These days it was hard to remain anonymous in the world, so it seemed she had sprung up out of nowhere.

That was the exact reason I was going to John's party. To find information on a person that was buried over eighteen years ago.

LYING IS INFINITELY EASIER when you use Lucifer as your alibi. Not even Tobias, Asher, and Olly, would dare call him to verify that we were going on a father-daughter vacation. They *had* given me a slightly skeptical look though.

On a scale of one to ten, this lie was right in the middle at a five or six. My lie wasn't hurting anyone but it would certainly piss Tobias off. Asher would be frustrated but then move on. Olly would see my point of view.

I pulled my car into the garage and breathed a sigh of relief. So far, operation *Who's My Mommy?*

was off to a great start. Who doesn't love lying to the men they love?

After turning off the alarm, I walked into the dark house, turning on lights. Besides the impromptu stay when I thought Asher was gone forever, I'd been gone for almost three months. I missed the freedom the house gave me, especially when Lucifer wasn't around. It might sometimes be lonely with a semi-absent father, but it was better than living with the staff members of your school.

This week away was just what I needed to refresh and try to regain my sanity. *Alone.* The word felt wrong somehow as it echoed in my head. Or maybe that was just my guilt.

I pulled out my phone and messaged my angels that I had made it. They were under the assumption that my dad was flying us to Hawaii. The thought of flying over the ocean angel-style gave me the heebie-jeebies and that should have been their first clue that I was pulling the wool over their eyes.

Asher was the first to respond. *Make sure to send us plenty of pictures of you in a bikini.*

I rolled my eyes. I should have said we were going somewhere cold instead of to Hawaii. I wasn't sure what they were going to do when they found out I deceived them. They cut me too much slack most of the time, but this might push them over the edge.

I needed to do this on my own, and they would just complicate matters. Walking into a party with three men, two of which were well into their twenties appearance-wise, would raise a lot of eyebrows. The attention would complicate my stealth-mode operation. At least that was what I kept telling myself.

Maybe this *was* a bad idea.

I carried my bag up to my old room and plopped down on the bed. Ava would arrive soon to get ready for the party. I was a bit nervous about John Junior and how much he knew about me. Had he been in Los Angeles when I was abducted and brought to the port?

I would soon find out just how much he knew when I showed up at his house uninvited. It wasn't like I could hide out once I was there. I had lots of friends and acquaintances, and word would spread through the party like wildfire.

My phone buzzed with a text from Ava and I practically flew down the stairs to let her in. It had only been three weeks since I last saw her, but when I opened the door it felt like it had been a lifetime. How can someone change so much in less than a month?

"Ava! What the hell?" I grabbed her arm and yanked her in the house, looking behind her. Clearly she'd been body snatched and it was possible the culprit was right behind her.

She let out a frustrated sigh and put her hands on her hips. I shut the door and turned to stare at her.

Ava had always been unassuming, wearing her long blond hair in a braid or ponytail. She dressed modestly by today's standards. Now she was sporting royal blue hair, styled in large curls that fell down her back. Her makeup was thick and her eyes rimmed with eyeliner and fake eyelashes. I had never once been able to get her to try them and here she was with falsies.

Her clothes were what concerned me most. Typically, for a party, she would wear jeans and a blouse. Maybe a dress if she wanted to dress up. But now, my best friend had on booty shorts over fishnet stockings and a corset-like top. Her boots looked like something a stripper might wear.

"You look great, but seriously, what the hell?" I was pretty sure it was April and not October. Maybe Halloween had moved to the Spring? In my sleep deprived state, I was tempted to pull out my phone to double check the date.

"It was time for a change. That's not what you're wearing, is it?" She scrunched up her nose at my pajama bottoms and hoodie I had changed into after class.

"Of course not. Time for a change? *Some* change." I moved towards the stairs, my mind still reeling over her drastic change in appearance. "So, who's the boy?"

"Why do you assume it's a boy?" She followed me, her heeled knee-high boots echoing in the empty room.

"A girl?" It had to be someone or something because she just wouldn't make that drastic a change to her appearance for no reason. None of her texts over the past three weeks said anything about dying her hair blue or going all hoochy mama. Her outfit was something *I* would wear.

"It's just because. Do I need a reason to dye my hair?" We entered my room and she sat in my desk chair. "While you're here, we should dye your hair. You'd look really good with red."

I snorted and pulled a pair of skinny jeans and a red crop top out of my bag. "I think my boyfriends would kill me."

"Even more reason to change your hair, spice things up a little. Not that they aren't spicy enough as it is. I mean, there are three of them." She propped her legs up on the desk and turned her head towards me. "Have you had two in you at once yet? You've had anal right?" She spewed questions like it was the Spanish Inquisition.

My eyes widened at the abrupt change in subject from her hair to my sex life. I changed into my clothes while considering my answer, although I wasn't sure I wanted to even go there with her. I told Ava almost everything, but had been keeping my sexual exploits with three men more private because I didn't think she'd want to hear anything about it.

She had barely had her first kiss, and now she was asking me about anal sex? I was sure she knew all about the birds and the bees, she was too smart not to, but she had never asked me details before.

"They haven't asked, so I haven't brought it up. It's not that I'm opposed to it though." Sleeping with multiple guys at once was still something so foreign to me. I felt like I was dreaming every time we were together.

Once Olly decided to join the mix, things would get even more interesting. Especially if my observation of the tiny spark between him and Asher was correct. I was anxiously awaiting that moment.

I walked into my bathroom and left the door open while I put on more make-up than I'd worn in months. Fake eyelashes felt incredibly strange after not wearing them for a while. I finished my look with a bright red lip.

"It's good to be back," I said, flipping the light off and grabbing my purse and jacket. "Let's roll."

"Heck yes! Are you drinking or smoking tonight? I kind of want to have a drink." Ava stood and headed for the door.

I grabbed her arm and stopped her. Ava never drank. What had happened to my best friend?

"Spill it. Now. Or I swear I will tie you to my bed until you tell me what's going on." I frowned at her and really examined her face. She didn't look like she was in pain or sad, but even I knew how easy it was to hide the pain within.

She bit her lip and seemed to be thinking about what she wanted to tell me. My heart dropped. I was losing my best friend by not being here. Maybe this change had started even earlier than the three weeks I'd been gone.

"Stanford rescinded my scholarship. I'm still waiting for them to decide if they're going to revoke my admissions." Tears formed in her eyes and she took a deep breath. "I was arrested."

I dropped her arm. "When? How? Holy shit, Ava." I sat down on the edge of my bed and looked up at her.

If anyone should have been arrested by this point in their life, it was me. They hadn't even arrested me for the joint in my locker. What had she done? Robbed a bank? Stolen all the blue hair dye from Sally's Beauty Supply?

She sat down next to me and put her face in her hands. I put my arm around her and tried to think of what to say. What do you say to someone who literally *never* got into trouble?

"Right after you went back to school. It's so embarrassing." She took her hands off her face and I grabbed her hand in support. "I broke into a house, but I don't even know why I did it. The whole night was kind of a blur. One second I was in my bedroom, studying, and the next I felt this over-whelming pull. So I followed where it led."

My eyebrows drew together at this odd story she was delivering. The last time she was at my house she had felt a strong pull towards a demon in my kitchen. I never did ask my dad what type of demon he was. Did he have something to do with this?

"I broke in through a window of the house but no one was there. There must have been a silent alarm because the next thing I knew I was being handcuffed and put in the back of a police car."

That still didn't explain why Ava decided to go all Clementine from *Eternal Sunshine of a Spotless Mind* and dye her hair blue. Her new look screamed 'look at me!'

"You didn't steal anything, did you?" I stood, keeping her hand clasped in mine and pulled her up from the bed.

"No, but it was a celebrity's house. I don't know how I got close enough to even break in. There were security guards and the gate was pretty tall. My parents are so disappointed in me and are making me help pay for my lawyer. I had to get a job and this," she gestured to herself, "is part of it. Let's just go. I don't want to talk about it anymore."

Ignoring her plea to drop the subject, I probed. "What job? You're not a stripper are you?"

She laughed. "No. There's this new bar and restaurant in downtown Santa Barbara called Blue Wave and it has a giant mermaid aquarium. I'm a mermaid. I get amazing tips."

I let out a sigh of relief that she wasn't taking off her clothes, at least not in the way I had thought, and hugged her before we left for John's house.

THE THING about high school parties in Montecito is that they are typically thrown by the most popular, richest of teenagers. Everyone who is anyone in the immediate area shows up and it is one big booze, drug, and fuck fest. Case in point, John Adamson's parties.

I parked my car in the lot next to John's estate. There were already dozens of cars parked in the dirt lot next door that had forever been vacant land. In fact, vacant lots surrounded all four sides of the house. I'd never thought much of it before, but now it piqued my curiosity.

We made our way through the side gate and into the backyard that already had drunken chicken fighting going on in the heated pool. The steam from the water made it look like something straight out of a horror movie right before someone gets killed.

"Danica fucking Deville, how the hell have you been? Heard you were sent to a military school or some bullshit. Rough," a guy named Brad said, slinging his arm around my shoulders. "John has some sweet ass devil's lettuce in the game room. You should check it out."

A grin spread across my face. I missed this crowd and how much they made me smile. Being surrounded by people that actually liked me, and at the very least tolerated me, was such a stark difference from being at the academy.

I followed Ava into the house where music was blaring from speakers and people were jumping around with their arms in the air. We made it to the kitchen and Ava grabbed a cup of some concoction that looked like punch but surely packed a punch of its own. I just grabbed a cup and filled it with water.

I was still reeling from what she had shared with me. It still wasn't clear what happened leading up to breaking into the house. Surely it couldn't have been so cut and dry. I'd have to probe her more once she had some alcohol in her.

My first order of business was to figure out where John was. I left Ava with a few friends and told her I was going to go mingle. Instead, I made my way to the game room where I knew John usually congregated with his inner circle and slipped inside.

The musky smell of Santa Barbara's finest weed hit my nostrils. I didn't love or hate the smell, but was glad the French doors leading outside were open to help dissipate the pungent odor. There were a few dozen people inside, lounging on couches and bar stools. A few people were using the single lane bowling alley and several were gathered around the pool table.

I glanced around and spotted John at the same time he spotted me. A large grin spread across his face and he rose from his spot on the couch and made his way over to me.

The last time I saw him he had blood running through his fingers as he held his broken nose. His nose looked better than it had before. Maybe a career in nose jobs was in my future.

"Dee! I'm surprised you have the balls to show your face in my house. I hope you're here to apologize for fucking up my nose." He grabbed my hips and put his lips against my ear to whisper. "We can go somewhere more private, unless you prefer an audience."

I shoved him away and resisted the urge to wrinkle my nose in disgust. He might be a stereotypical rich pretty boy, but he was sorely lacking in the personality department. It made him ugly.

"Why would I apologize when your nose looks so much better now?" I smirked and turned to walk away but he grabbed my arm. I stopped and turned back to face him.

"You're lucky you moved away," he said, his mouth in a tight line instead of the smile he was previously wearing. The sound of his voice held a threat. He let go of my arm with a shove. "Enjoy the party."

I watched as he made his way back to the couch and didn't spare me another glance. *Perfect.*

I left the room and made my way to the staircase leading upstairs. It was strictly off-limits but it was doubtful anyone would say anything if they saw me slip up the stairs.

I tried several doors, finding guest rooms and bathrooms. The room I assumed was John Senior's office had an electronic lock on it. It was the only door on the hall that had it and it was the only one locked.

I slipped into the guest room next to it and made my way to the French door leading out onto the upstairs terrace that spanned the entire back of the house. I was hoping what I thought was the office had a similar door.

It seemed a bit ridiculous that someone would have a state-of-the-art lock on an inner door, but then ignore the fact that the outer door was covered in glass panes. The lack of outer stair access gave a false sense of security.

I examined the door and pulled the lock picking tools I had bought on Amazon out of my purse. I had practiced on my own door at the academy, and after several YouTube videos, I was efficient as a burglar. You really could learn to do anything on the Internet. Why did I need school?

It was almost too easy to pop the locks on the door and I waited for twenty knives to fly at me or an alarm to sound. When nothing happened, I moved inside the room that was all wood accents. It smelled faintly of sweet cigar smoke. I pulled out my cell phone and turned on the flashlight.

I started at the bookshelves and skimmed the titles. Most were medical books with one shelf devoted to Stephen King. Of course he would be a Stephen King fan. He had Stephen King vibes written all over him.

I wasn't sure what I was looking for. I just knew that if he had something, it was going to be in his office. All bad guys kept important information in their office. It was in the rule book of being a bad guy.

I opened a few drawers and cabinets at the bottom of the built-in bookcases and found old medical instruments in boxes, but not much else. He probably had a safe hidden behind a picture. I looked around but the walls were bare.

Where would he keep information about private patients?

I went to the desk and tried the drawers. The only one that opened was the center one which just had a bunch of junk in it. I sifted through it and then turned my attention to the drawer that was the size of a file cabinet drawer. I picked the lock and pulled it open. All the files were labeled with initials. I wasn't sure he would have files on any of us, but one could hope.

I located them easily, all three the same colored red folders right next to each other. I quickly checked inside to make sure I had the correct ones before shoving them into the waistband of my jeans and zipping up my leather jacket.

It was so tempting to look at them right then

and there, but I was already pushing my luck being in the office for so long.

I exited the same way I'd entered and turned the bottom lock so at least then it wouldn't seem too obvious the room had been broken into. I made my way back through the guest room and down the stairs into the fray of the party.

I found Ava in a group of people, her eyes glossy from drinking.

"Hey, I forgot something in my car. I'm going to run out and grab it." She hugged me and kissed my cheek. She was definitely feeling the effects of whatever was in the punch. When I got back from my car I was going to have to cut her off and then interrogate her to find out more about her break-in and her new job. Something was fishy about it, and not just because she was moonlighting as a mermaid.

Out in the lot there were a few people making out against the sides of cars, but otherwise it was quiet besides the faint sound of the ocean. I slid the files out from my jacket and locked them in the glove box. It was tempting to sit in the car and go through them, but Ava probably was in need of a babysitter.

I somehow felt responsible for whatever was going on with her.

I shut the door and turned around, only to bump right into someone's chest. I stepped back to meet the angry eyes of John, with two of his friends flanking his sides. I turned to run but his two friends grabbed me by the arms and shoved me against my car. John stepped close to me. I could smell the stench of weed coming off his clothes.

"You shouldn't have come back. You know the drill, right? Nothing personal." He spoke in a low voice that sent shivers down my spine and a few small drops of his saliva landed on my face. There was no amount of washing that would ever get the feeling off.

"Fuck you, you piece of-" My words were cut off as his fist connected with my gut, causing me to double over as far as the two goons holding me would allow.

I tried to kick out at him, but his friends shifted their bodies to hold my legs against my car with theirs. I let out a scream, but it was useless. Everyone knew that if John invited you to be a part of his band of merry drug dealers and you refused, he'd beat the shit out of you. I really had been hoping it was an urban legend, but who was I kidding? He'd probably kick an infant if it refused. I'd made it ten times worse by turning him down publicly and punching the fucker in the nose.

He sent another punch to my side and my eyes blurred as tears filled them. I spat at him, my saliva landing on his jawline. He wiped it off with a disgusted look on his face.

"Bitch." He slapped my face. The shape of his hand burned into my cheek.

"You aren't going to get away with this," I managed to get out through clenched teeth.

John threw his head back and laughed like Jack Nicholson in *The Shining*. I may have pissed my pants a little at the menacing sound.

"What do you guys think? Should I fuck up her face like she did mine? It's really too bad. She's such a gorgeous girl." He trailed his index finger down the side of my face and bopped my nose with it. I shivered in revulsion at his touch. This was going to hurt.

His fist connected with the center of my face, snapping my head back. My eyes slammed shut and warm liquid filled my nose and started seeping out. He then threw a punch at my chest that left me gasping for breath.

The two men that had ahold of my arms let me go and I fell to the ground, my palms scraping on the rough surface of the dirt. With one last kick to my stomach, John stepped away, laughing.

"I'm taking it easy on you, Dee. I hope you appreciate my leniency. If it were anyone else, it'd be so much worse." He squatted down next to me and patted my head. "I do hope you enjoyed my party. Don't let me see you at my house again."

With that, they turned and left me bleeding next to my car.

Chapter Two

The mission had gone smashingly. A fist smashing right into my face. It had to be karma for keeping this from those who were supposed to be guarding me.

Guarding me from what exactly was still up for debate. I didn't need babysitters to steal harmless files, did I?

I had considered calling the police, but what would I tell them? Hell, he and his father had been arrested and gotten off scot-free. They probably had the cops on a leash.

This was the second time in my life I had the shit beaten out of me. The first time was when the Fallen kidnapped me. I didn't really remember much because I was in and out of consciousness. Olly healed me before I could fully wake up and process the pain.

The pain from John's beating still had me

feeling intensely sorry for myself on Sunday. My face and bruises hadn't looked that bad on Friday night, but now everything was blue and dark purple. It was going to be hard to hide the evidence.

Ava stayed with me Friday and Saturday. I had been unable to get anything else out of her about her new look and job. I hoped she wasn't headed down the same path of bad decisions I had been down.

I was alone again. In hindsight, going to the party was a mistake. I hadn't thought he'd actually beat me, maybe just give me shit about breaking his nose. I should've known he had no moral compass. What a jackass.

I hadn't even bothered getting the files out of my car. It took too much effort to go up and down the stairs. With Ava being gone, I had to hobble down the stairs to get food. I made sure to grab the files out of my glovebox.

Taking them back to my room, I sat on my bed and stared at the blood red folders. None of them were thick, with only a few documents in each. I ran my hand over one of the folders. It was Lucifer's.

I lifted the corner. There was only one piece of paper inside. I stood and stared down at the folder. If I looked in the files, I would know more about myself, hopefully. I might also find out things I *didn't* want to know about myself. It was hard enough being the daughter of the devil, but now there was a great probability my mother was right up there on the list of most hated too.

No one ever talked about *the* Lilith. She was mysterious. She was deadly. Some internet websites said she stole babies. Some said she was a demon. Movies and TV shows often portrayed her as an evil vampire queen. A few sources proclaimed she was the representation of the independent woman and should be revered.

It was possible the prophecy wasn't even true and all of my worrying was for nothing. It did seem a bit ridiculous on second thought, but archangels didn't make shit up. Tobias confirmed that Michael had, in fact, said that Lilith and Lucifer were the creator's biggest regrets.

What did that make me then? A double regret?

I lowered to my knees on the floor next to the bed and lay my chin on crossed arms. Lucifer's file would be the easiest to start with. He was an angel, of that I was sure.

I pulled the folder towards me and opened it, revealing a simple document.

Name: Lucifer
Alias: Michael Deville
Blood type: Nonhuman; Celestial 100%
Date of birth: Unknown

Under his vital information was a paragraph explaining his blood's reactions to introduced antigens and substances. Most of what was listed was written in code. There was one that had a plus sign next to it but the series of letters and numbers didn't reveal what it was.

How John even got a sample of my father's blood was beyond me. My dad guarded his blood like the Queen's Guard guards Buckingham Palace.

I closed the file and set it to the side. I grabbed my mother's file next and stared at it. What if she was human and died a normal death during childbirth? What if she wasn't even my mother and she had baby-snatched me from a real human and implanted me into her womb?

Now, that was a Syfy movie waiting to happen.

Name: Lilith
Alias: Lilith Judith Gardner
Blood type: Nonhuman; Demonoid 100%
Date of birth: Unknown
Alias DOB: April 30, 1975

The first paper in the file was similar to Lucifer's, several codes for antigens were listed. One had a plus sign next to it. I wish I knew what it meant.

I stared at the page for a long time before turning to the next where an autopsy report done by Doctor Adamson detailed the date of death and the unknown cause of massive blood loss during a routine cesarean section.

I shut the folder and sat it on top of my father's. My chin trembled and tears blurred my vision. My father had been duped into loving a demon.

I sucked in a breath of air and let it out slowly. My file was staring back at me. It had more than just two papers in it.

How could this even happen? How could my mother be a demon?

I opened the file.

Name: Danica Marie Deville
Blood type: Nonhuman; Inconclusive Celestial, Inconclusive Demonoid
Date of birth: January 20, 2001

The same tests were run on my blood, with several having plus signs. I flipped the page to a detailed list of tests run on my blood to determine the percentages of my lineage, but every test repeated the same word "inconclusive." It figured that even my blood couldn't pass a test.

I grumbled in frustration. Leaving the folder open on my bed, I made my way downstairs again to watch television. My brain couldn't handle anymore digging into my mother or into what I was. My brain certainly didn't want to let go of the fact that I might be half demon though.

Is that why I didn't have angel wings?

Is that why I was such a fuck up at everything I did?

I fell asleep on the couch, my nightmares worse than ever. When I woke, I didn't feel rested. In fact, I felt like I hadn't slept at all, and my breast hurt and my nose throbbed.

I trudged upstairs, my feet dragging on the ground and hopped in the shower. The hot water did little to ease my mind or the aches from being beaten. There was a weariness that came with the exhaustion that had slowly been building in my body over the past few weeks.

I should have been happy. I should have been excited for this next phase in my life with my three angels. Instead, I was petrified that I would sprout horns or go ape-shit and kill someone. Demons were not the soft and cuddly type. What if it was like in the movies with werewolves and one day I just woke up growly and lusting after blood?

I had so many questions that I didn't know who to ask. Lucifer would probably know a lot of the answers, but how could I tell him that Lily was Lilith? At least, that's what all signs were pointing to.

Hell, maybe he already knew.

I threw on my purple terry cloth robe and opened the bathroom door. I nearly jumped out of my skin seeing my father sitting on the side of my bed looking through the papers I had left there. He was lucky I hadn't decided to walk out of my bathroom naked.

"Dad, what are you doing here?" I asked,

rushing over to the bed and starting to gather the papers and folders.

He didn't look up from the papers he was examining. He just sat there and stared at them in his hand in silence. I gathered what he didn't have in his hands and plopped next to him. I didn't know if I was more anxious about him seeing the papers or seeing the bruises that covered my face. At least he couldn't see the ones covering my torso.

"Please say something." My hands were shaking and I felt my eyes burning.

This was not how I wanted to tell him that Lily might have been a lie. Had she even loved him? He didn't talk about her often, but when he did it was evident he had loved her so damn much. When he did talk to me about her, he always had a wistful look in his eyes, which was always odd to see on his typically stoic face.

The possibility of her deceiving him was inconceivable. It would break his heart all over again. How do you mend the devil's heart? It was impossible. It would ruin him.

"Oliver called me last night. He wanted to know if on the last night in Hawaii I would be okay with them coming to join us. He said they wanted it to be a surprise. Why did you tell your boyfriends that you're in Hawaii? They're supposed to protect you. How can they protect you when you're putting your nose in places it doesn't belong?" He lifted his head to look at me then, his expression changing immediately from sad to angry.

He lifted his hand to my face and ran his fingers along my swollen nose, busted lip, and the dark bruise around my eye. I looked down at my hands as a tear slid down my cheek.

"Who did this to you?" His voice held a note of violence. He was pissed and he hadn't even seen the rest of my body.

"Just let it be. It's done and over with." I stood, wincing at the pain in my side with the quick movement. "It's my own fault."

I made my way to my bag that Ava had kindly placed on my desk and dug out some comfortable clothes. I went into the bathroom and changed, coming back out in pajama pants and one of Asher's T-shirts.

"Let me see your stomach." Lucifer was still sitting on my bed, papers in his hand. He must have remained in that same position while I changed.

I twisted my mouth in concern. He paid too much attention. Of course he would know that my face was not the only thing that had been beaten to a pulp.

I sighed and stood in front of him, lifting my shirt to reveal my stomach. He took a sharp inhale of breath and my head swam as the room filled with anger. He was going to murder John, I was sure of it. Maybe he deserved it.

"Danica Marie. I'm going to ask you again, who

did this?" The initial swell of his anger receded a bit and he stared up at me.

I pulled my shirt back down and gingerly sat back down next to him. All the movement was starting to make me feel stiff. Instead of telling him directly who had beaten the shit out of me, I changed the subject back to the files.

"I needed to do this on my own," I said gesturing to the files on the bed. "I had to know, to confirm it. Did you know?"

He placed the papers he had been holding for an eternity behind him and then ran a hand through his hair. "I did not. How did you get these files? Is that how you were beaten?"

"I broke into John Adamson's office while John Junior was having his annual Spring break party." I played with the hem of my shirt. "Are you mad?"

"I'm not mad. I'm disappointed in you. You should've told me this sooner. How long have you known?" He stood from the bed and walked over to my dresser, flipping open my jewelry box.

"About three weeks. Michael told Tobias that we couldn't tell you. Something about it might make you go crazy," I said softly. It had seemed like logical reasoning at the time, but now I wasn't so sure.

He made an annoyed noise in his throat. He and Michael weren't the best of friends.

He returned to sit next to me with a necklace in his hand. It was a pendant necklace he had given my mother that had a lily encrusted with the tiniest of diamonds. He gazed down at it in the palm of his hand as if he were trudging through a memory.

"The papers in my file say I'm angel and demon but then say it's all inconclusive. What does that mean?" My voice was shaking.

"It means nothing. You're still you. Just because you know this new information about yourself doesn't change who you are in your heart. Does it?" He held out the necklace and I opened my palm for him to drop it into. I wrapped my fist around it, my knuckles turning white, the pendant digging into my skin.

My tears were falling freely now. My dad pulled me into a hug as gently as possible, his hand rubbing my back. I hadn't wanted it to happen this way, him finding out about Lilith. Now I was glad it had because it was just us. The both of us would deal with the deceit together.

After several minutes of silence, he finally spoke. "What should I tell your boyfriends? I told Oliver I'd get back to him. If you won't tell me who beat you up, maybe you'll tell them."

Shit. I almost forgot about that. What was I going to tell them? Now there was no hiding the fact that Hawaii had been a fabrication. Maybe my dad could heal my bruises. They would never have to know. I was too scared to ask him to add to the lie.

"I should just let you take care of it. Anything

else going on that I should know about?" He raised his eyebrows.

"Well, now that you mention it, Ava got arrested for breaking into a house." A small smile turned up the corners of Lucifer's lips. "She told me she was at home and she felt the overwhelming urge to go there, but doesn't really remember much."

Lucifer's face fell and he stood abruptly. "I need to go."

"What is it? Is it that demon that was in our kitchen three weeks ago? Ava thought she was in love with him. What kind of demon is he?" I spewed my questions out in quick succession, already sensing he was about to take off.

Whatever it was, it wasn't good. He seemed panicked.

He grabbed the stack of papers and folders, and without another word, he vanished. I wished he would have healed me before he left.

THEY SAY honesty is the best policy, but I'm not so sure about that. Did I really need to tell them that I lied to them or what I had found out? Maybe I'd just tell them some of the truth. I didn't plan on telling them I was half demon. I could barely tell myself.

I took a deep breath and pressed the green call button on Olly's contact information. He'd probably take the news the best. He could have the honor of telling the other two.

"Dani! How's paradise?" Olly answered, his voice full of excitement.

Now I really felt like my demon blood was at work inside of me. Why did I think going all secret agent was a good idea? I was fine, up until Olly's cheerful voice smacked me back to reality, and the fact that they were angels and I wasn't hit me across the face.

Fuck. I needed a drink. Maybe ten drinks.

"Hey there. What are you up to?" I laid back on my bed and stared at the ceiling fan as it slowly spun round and round.

My stomach muscles pulled tight and I twisted my face to keep a sound from escaping. I needed to go get my ice packs out of the freezer. The hopes of my dad coming back and healing me were diminishing. My calls and texts to him sat unanswered.

"Just up here on the roof with Tobias, helping Asher with his garden. Here, let me put you on speaker." Before I could object, I heard fumbling. "I've never planted anything before. It's pretty neat, but dirty."

"I'll show you dirty," I heard Asher say in the background. "Hey, Danica! Where are those bikini pics? Ow!" He grunted like he had been hit.

"Excuse him, he has no respect. How are you doing? Getting lots of rest I hope." Tobias, always the concerned one. He had good reasons to always be concerned about me. I acted first, thought later. Story of my life.

"I want to preface this conversation by saying that I'm sorry. Lucifer told me Olly called." I pulled up my shirt as I spoke and looked at the bruises.

"Damn. Who would have thought the devil wouldn't be able to keep a secret," Olly said.

"I'm not in Hawaii." I flinched before I could even hear their reactions.

In my mind, I could see them react. Tobias would stop whatever he was doing and stare at the phone in disbelief before putting his hands on his hips. He'd then give the phone his 'teacher' look. The one that sends chills to the very depths of souls.

Asher would hesitate for a second before continuing whatever he was doing, avoiding the anxiety a confrontation might bring.

Olly, well he was the wildcard of the group, more of a Switzerland type. That was the reason I had called him and not the other two.

"Where are you then?" Olly asked, uncertainty in his voice.

"My house. There was never a Hawaii trip." Silence. Complete silence. "There was something I needed to take care of."

"You lied to us? Why would you do that?" I was surprised that Olly was the one who spoke, hurt evident in his voice. He was supposed to be my Switzerland.

I let out a sigh and winced as I sat up against my headboard, the bruises on my torso protesting. "I couldn't exactly take three angels to a high school party, could I? Plus if John saw Asher, he might have known I was up to something."

"What do you mean if John saw me? What did you do?" Asher was closer to the phone now, his voice coming through the speaker loud and clear.

"I think the more important question is why she lied just to go to a high school party by herself," Tobias said.

"I broke into John Senior's office and helped myself to some medical files." I bit my lip and held the phone slightly away from my ear, already knowing by now that I was going to get a reaction.

"You did what?" Tobias's raised voice sounded like he was about to have a heart attack. "I thought we had all agreed to wait for Michael to give us directions on our next steps."

"Plans change," I mumbled into the phone. My life had certainly changed.

"We're coming," Tobias said and then the line went dead before I could protest.

My heart thudded in my chest, making my bruises ache even more. John didn't kill me, but I was pretty sure I was about to die at the hands of Tobias.

Twenty minutes later, they knocked on the door. Having angel wings had its perks, like lightning fast travel.

I slid off the barstool I had been waiting on and walked to the door like I was marching to my reckoning. Or more like hobbling towards it.

When I opened the door, they stood there with bags in hand. I met their gazes head on, because there was no hiding my swollen nose and the bruised flesh on my face.

They didn't look happy to begin with, and as they took in my face, their eyes widened. The frowns on their faces grew deeper the longer they stared.

I moved out of the way and they walked in without a word.

I shut the door behind them, then made my way to the couch and sat down gingerly. I felt like I had done one thousand sit-ups. Maybe if I had, I would have had abs of steel and John would have been the one in pain.

Their silence was killing me. Asher sat on my left and Olly on my right. Tobias sat in the armchair.

"What the hell happened?" Tobias finally asked. It was hard to tell what he was feeling. My guess was that there was anger simmering under the surface, along with concern.

"To make a long story short, this was three months in the making," I said, gesturing to my face with a sigh. I looked at the coffee table in front of me, wishing it was a portal away from the scrutinizing gazes.

Olly brought his hands to my face and they began to glow. Warmness spread across my cheeks, nose, and around my eyes. The dull ache that had settled across it slowly ebbed and my face was left feeling like I had just had a relaxing facial at a spa.

"Did that John kid do this?" Asher asked, balling his fists in his lap.

His eyes kept darting around the room, as if he was looking for something. The last thing I needed was for any of them to kill John. We all knew that killing a human without an order would mean falling as an angel.

I nodded. "You don't need to go and defend my honor."

I lifted my shirt and Asher's eyes widened. He clenched his jaw. Olly frowned down at me and placed his hands over my bruised ribs, healing them. I bit my lip and raised my shirt to expose my breast.

"I'm going to kill that motherfucker." Asher stood and walked out of the house, slamming the door behind him. I didn't know where he thought he was going; it wasn't like he knew where John lived.

I looked back at the door. I hadn't meant to set off Asher. He had been doing so well lately. Just another fuck up to add to my ever-growing list.

Tobias moved to the couch next to me, taking my hand. Olly healed the bruise on my breast before placing a kiss on it. Thank God it was healed; it had been the worst of them all.

"I'll go make sure he's all right," Olly said, standing and walking out the door.

"He could've killed you, and for what? Was risking your life really worth what you were after?" Tobias's eyes searched mine as if trying to understand me and my less than stellar choices.

Sometimes I didn't even understand my choices, and I was the one who made them.

I leaned back on the cushions and shut my eyes. Was it worth it to reveal myself? It was, but it wasn't. I was torn into a million little pieces. I was inconclusive, whatever that meant.

"My dad took the files." I left it at that. No need to get into specifics until I knew more.

I felt Tobias shift next to me and then he pulled me towards him. I kept my eyes shut because I didn't want to see the disappointment on his face. He ran his fingers through my hair and kissed my forehead.

"So Lucifer knows now? Michael warned us not to tell him. At least not yet."

"There was an autopsy report for her. My dad buried her, or at least he thinks he did. I wonder..." I stopped speaking as the thought came to my mind. I must be more demon than angel, because no angel would consider digging up a grave.

Would they?

"If you're thinking about what I think you're

thinking about... No," Tobias said firmly, reading my mind. Or maybe he read the look on my face.

"We'd know for sure. Well, at least that she really isn't dead. Lilith or not, I need to know. Wouldn't you want to know if it was your mother?" I opened my eyes and his brown eyes stared sparkling back at me.

He leaned forward and brushed his lips over mine. I pulled him closer and deepened the kiss, my mouth opening and allowing his tongue to explore. His lips moved to my jaw and slowly kissed their way to my ear.

"I think that, later, a spanking is in order," he said before sucking the skin right under my ear. My nipples hardened and rubbed against my T-shirt. He sure talked a big spanking game, but had yet to bend me over his lap. I wasn't opposed to the idea; the thought mostly made me giggly.

Tobias moved back to my lips and stood, placing a knee on the couch and then straddled me. I moaned into his mouth. The weight of his body on top of mine increased the wetness already forming between my legs.

There was something so intimate about him being on top of me like he was. No wonder guys liked to be straddled; it was fucking hot.

My hands slipped under his shirt and ran up and down his spine. He made a noise in his throat and moved his lips to my neck, suckling the skin just shy of leaving a hickey.

"We're gone for five minutes and he's already trying to get in her pants," I heard Asher mumble as the front door clicked shut. Olly chuckled in response.

Tobias continued to kiss my neck and moved a hand under my shirt, cupping a breast in his hand. He moved his thumb across the hard nipple and I shuddered with pleasure. I glanced over as Asher and Olly sat down as if we weren't dry humping in front of them.

It still blew my mind that they were content with sharing me. I wouldn't be able to share them with another woman, that was for sure. Did that make me a hypocrite?

"Olly and I have decided that John deserves to get his ass kicked. He'll do the ass kicking part since I can't risk being sent back to the high court. Are you two in or are you going to stay and suck each other's faces off?" Asher had an amused lilt to his voice. It was nice to hear considering he had left the room in a murderous rage not long ago.

I groaned as Tobias pulled his hand away and looked over at Asher. "Can't it wait?"

"Can it *wait*? I am vengeance," Asher said in a lower register. He stood back up from his place on the couch.

Tobias made a strangled noise in his throat and moved off of me. "Well, now I have to go since you think you're Batman and just ruined the mood. I sometimes feel like a babysitter to grown ass men." I really felt like he should have added "and a woman."

"Well, if you really feel that way, then I guess you can be my Alfred, Olly can be my Robin, and Danica can be my Catwoman."

"I don't know about that." I scrunched my nose.

Asher grabbed my hand and pulled me off the couch. He planted a wet kiss on my lips that I had to wipe off with my hand. I both loved and hated when he did that. "Alfred, why don't you make us some dinner? We need sustenance for all the ass kicking and fucking we're going to do tonight."

I lightly smacked Asher's chest and squirmed out of his arms. He had been very playful lately and the troubled look that was usually in his eyes had lessened. It was definitely still there though, like when he walked in and saw me beaten.

"There's no food in the house, unless you want hot pockets or a sandwich." I was slightly embarrassed by my food selection. It wasn't like I'd had time to go to the grocery store. What I had was what Ava picked up.

"Then what have you been eating?" Tobias sounded concerned. If he didn't mellow out he was going to give himself a coronary or a head of gray hair.

"Hot pockets, cereal, sandwiches, and takeout. The usual."

Olly jumped up and faced Tobias. "Let's go out to eat then. Please, *Dad*, we never go out to eat!"

Tobias lunged for him and put him in a head-lock. "Take it back or I'll spank your ass too." Tobias made a move to try to smack him on the ass and he twisted to avoid his hand, laughing hysterically.

Were they all on something? They were supposed to be mad at me for going rogue and getting my ass kicked, not acting like teenage boys. I half expected to get a lecture on the finer points of thinking and using common sense.

"So you guys aren't mad at me?" My question caused Tobias to finally let Olly go.

"There's no use in being mad. It's done and over with," Asher said, sitting on the arm of the couch. "Now go get changed so we can go eat."

Chapter Three

Asher

I knew the second my feelings escalated with Oliver. I had just damn near had a panic attack over Danica's bruised body. I loved the girl to pieces, would give my life for her again if necessary, but she was going to give me an ulcer.

Not that I could get an ulcer now.

The result of the exposé of her bruises was that I had badly wanted to punch or destroy something. My heart had been pounding at an uncomfortable level and my body was thrumming for a release, and not a sexual one. Shit would be so much simpler if *that* was the case.

My eyes had darted from the television, to the decorative bowl in the center of the coffee table, and then to the lamp on the end table. All prime stock for smashing to pieces.

Instead of destroying the living room, I had rushed out of the house and punched the shit out of the brick siding. I hadn't been able to stop myself. I'd needed to feel something other than the panic in my chest.

The impact had brought me back to reality, but in the process it also did a number on my hand. My skin was ripped to shreds, blood seeping out of my knuckles. It fucking hurt like it had gone through a meat grinder.

I was cradling my hand, trying to calm myself down, when I felt Oliver touch my shoulder to alert me to his presence. He was as silent as a ninja when he wanted to be.

His touch was gentle, just like *all* his touches were.

Fuck him and his gentle touches.

They did something to me, and not just ease my anxiety. Every time he touched me it was like he was touching my soul or some shit. My soul was already confused as it was. He just made it worse.

His touching had increasingly gotten more and more frequent and definitely not just at night when he was keeping away my anxiety. He'd touch me anytime he was near. His favorite move was brushing his arm against me as he passed or as he stood at my side.

And damn if I didn't start touching him too. I found myself moving closer to him when we were in the same room. Purposefully placing myself next to him on a couch or at a table.

I never really considered a relationship with a man before. Hell, I never considered being part of a polyamorous relationship either. Yet here we all were. There was a strange connection between us, where we felt drawn to each other.

Oliver was not my type at all. He was all doe-eyed and virginal, while I had the experience of at least ten men. I didn't know how to be gentle or take things slow. Hell, I would have slept with Danica on our first date if he and his idiot friend hadn't interrupted us.

"Let me see your hand." The fucker didn't even wait for my response but took it anyway, making my pulse speed up. He was supposed to ease my anxiety, not increase it.

I had my self-healing ability back, but it didn't exactly work like it was supposed to. I could heal a hangnail and that was my limit. Healing took complete mental and physical awareness, which I was running low on. I might have gotten my wings back, but normalcy still eluded me.

But at least I could fly again.

His hands started glowing the color of a setting sun, and I watched as my skin knitted back together and the bruising faded away. It was a handy trick to be able to heal others. Archangels were born to do it; the rest of us could only heal ourselves unless we went through years of study. It involved a lot of inner peace and positive thoughts. No wonder I couldn't even heal myself.

He kept ahold of my hand and pulled me towards the water hose attached to the house. He turned on the spicket and grabbed the end of the hose, running the cold water over my hand to rinse the blood off.

I didn't speak as he held my hand in his palm and rubbed his thumb over my knuckles, working the blood out of the creases. He was so focused, his blue eyes sparkling as he worked.

I felt like a fucking chick with hearts in my eyes when I was around him. When he and Tobias showed up on my rooftop earlier in the afternoon, I had seriously looked down at myself and regretted the ripped and dirty work clothes I was wearing. It was similar to how I had felt the first time I had Danica over to my house. The need to make a good impression was strong.

Punching a wall was probably not making a good impression, but he continued to come to me, to lock the demons back in their cages.

It was taking an awfully long time for him to clean my hand. I should have helped, but was content with him touching my hand in such an intimate way.

Where the fuck did this guy come from anyways? He had been a complete bastard to Danica and then did an abrupt one-eighty, seemingly overnight. If it had been anyone else I would have questioned their intentions, but Oliver was horribly naïve.

That was why I decided that it wasn't just Danica who needed protection, but him too. I would protect him from the world. However, I wasn't willing to protect him from the true threat. *Me.*

"I want to kick that guy's ass," I finally said. I had been wracking my brain for what to say after my epic meltdown of bloody proportions. "Who beats the shit out of a woman like that?"

A beaten woman was what had caused me to fall in the first place. I had snapped at the sight of her in the hallway of an apartment building I was a security guard at. My mission was explicit: get her to a battered women's shelter, file a police report. Instead, when the man had come out of the apartment after her, I had beaten the shit out of him. That wouldn't have been a problem but then I threw him off the fifth-floor balcony.

I can't say I regretted my decision.

Olly made a non-committal noise in his throat, never taking his eyes off my hand. "You can't beat him up, it's too risky. I'll do it."

I snorted and pulled my hand away, drying it on my jeans. He wasn't a violent person. His words surprised me.

Olly rinsed his own hands off then turned off the water, hanging the hose back up.

"Do you even know how to fight?" I teased. He

was much more of a lover than a fighter. He saved cockroaches for God's sake. Who saves *those?*

"I'm more into using a sword." He met my eyes and winked. What the hell was the wink for? Was he joking about his dick?

"Let me see your hand again just to make sure I healed it all the way," he said, reaching towards me again. I was pretty sure he knew he had, it was just another instance of him wanting to touch me.

I complied and he took my hand in his, gently probing the knuckles before turning my hand over and rubbing his thumb across the palm.

Fuck, that felt good. And fuck if I didn't want to kiss the motherfucker, but instead, I pulled my hand away.

"We should get back inside," I said, turning towards the door before he could touch me again.

AFTER CHANGING, we decided on a seafood restaurant on the water in Santa Barbara, since Oliver had never had seafood before. The four of us had never all gone out together, at least not to relax, and it was long overdue. With everything that had been happening, going on dates was pretty low on our priorities list.

Besides, we were long past what I would consider dating. We were right in the trenches of a committed relationship. All four of us.

We'd been through a lot. Danica and Oliver getting abducted. Oliver being forced to heal angels so they could be drained more frequently. Then there was the whole situation of my soul floating around like a jellyfish in a never-ending black abyss.

I thought being Fallen was bad, but being a lost soul was infinitely worse. There I was, for weeks, just floating in a dark void with only my thoughts as company. I thought my memories were bad now, but with no outlet like alcohol, violence, or sex, I had been a fucking mess.

Now that I had my angel wings back, things weren't much better. It's not like my memories could be erased because now they were so intertwined with who I was. Really, the only benefit was the wings; who wouldn't want to be able to fly? Traffic sucked a pair of hairy balls.

I slid into a chair next to a plexiglass wall, the sandy beach and ocean on the other side. The sun was just starting to go down and the waiters were lighting the outdoor heaters spread around the eating area.

Oliver slid into the seat next to me and placed the placemat and crayons he had grabbed at the hostess station in front of him. His old friends must have never taken him off campus much, judging by the way he was enthralled with every new experience. Coloring included.

We all watched as he emptied out the small box of four crayons and then looked up at us.

"You guys sure you don't want to color? I can go get you some. The hostess said adults can color too." He made me smile. Hell, he made us all smile.

I nudged his arm. "I'll pass, but make sure you bring that back with us and I'll hang it on my fridge, right beside your finger painting."

Oliver narrowed his eyes at me as the other two laughed. It was fun to tease him. I bet he would be fun to tease in the bedroom too. Not that I was thinking about it. Not at all.

"They sell adult coloring books. It's no different than me doodling," Danica said, shrugging. Oliver smiled at her and she winked.

"You and your doodles. You don't even need to put your name on your papers anymore, I just know which one belongs to you." Tobias opened his menu and took a drink of his water. "I want some oysters."

"Yuck. Aren't those raw?" I watched as Oliver started to shade in the pineapple in the picture. It was some kind of house for cartoon characters.

"Angel baby, can I order for you?" I asked, looking right at Oliver, who wasn't even looking at his menu yet. Knowing him, he had somehow already read the menu without even opening it. "You order the weirdest crap."

He'd probably order a plate of lemon wedges or some shit. He put the crayon down and cocked his head to the side with an incredulous look on his face.

"I do not. Food is food. Who cares what I eat?"

Last week when we ordered Chinese takeout, he had ordered brown rice. Who just eats brown rice? Brown rice tastes like cardboard.

The guy was as tall as the Jolly Green Giant and was built like an Adonis. He needed more than just rice, cantaloupe, and cookies. Sure he'd eat other things on occasion, but the list of Oliver approved foods was shorter than my dick. It was like he was scared of food, which was a shame. Seafood was going to really test his taste buds.

The restaurant did have a kids' selection, but damn if I was going to let him order macaroni and cheese and a corn dog.

The waitress arrived and raised her eyebrows at Oliver, who had just picked his crayon back up after staring me down. I couldn't blame her for the inquisitive look she was giving him, but I wanted to ask her what she was staring at. I was allowed to judge and tease him; he had seen my ass naked.

Danica and Tobias placed their orders.

"And for you, sir?" She looked down at me and made a show of running her eyes down what she could see of me before they landed back on my face.

Danica cleared her throat and was glaring daggers at the waitress. I hadn't even paid attention to the waitress up until this point, but judging by the smirk on Tobias's face, she had done the same to him.

"We'll both have the seafood pasta." I handed her the menus.

"She just openly eye-fucked all three of you," Danica said as soon as the waitress was out of earshot.

"You sound jealous," Tobias teased. "Women—or men—are allowed to check us out, aren't they?"

She made a strangled noise. "Not when they look like her."

I put my chin on my fist and stared across the table at her. Something was off about her tonight. I couldn't read people very well, but she seemed suddenly self-conscious. She was slightly hunched in her seat and had a frown across her face.

She was like that before the waitress even ogled us. It was unlike her and I didn't like it.

"She's got nothing on you. So what, she checked us out? You should see it as a compliment of your fine taste in men." I reached across the table and she took my hand. "What's going on with you?"

"Nothing," she answered quickly and squeezed my hand. "I guess I'm just PMSing."

I decided to drop it because I didn't want to touch *that* with a ten-foot pole. Tobias changed the subject and started rambling about the Dodgers.

When our appetizer arrived, Oliver's eyes nearly bugged out of his head as he examined the grand seafood platter Tobias had ordered to share. It was a sight to behold with oysters, shrimp, lobster, and crab.

"It looks like snot." He held a raw oyster in a half shell in his hand and the cocktail fork in the other. "You want me to *eat* this? What if I vomit or die? It could have worms in it."

"Have you been looking at a lot of snot lately? *Jesus.* You aren't going to vomit or die. I doubt an oyster is going to take you out. Look, Dani isn't vomiting *or* dying." I showed him how to make sure the oyster was sliding around in the shell and then tipped it into my mouth. "See? Easy."

"Can I put ketchup on it?" He eyed the oyster with uncertainty. A few people at another table were looking at him with amusement. He wasn't exactly being quiet. I was struggling not to grab his jaw and force the damn thing down his throat like he was a dog in need of his medicine.

"That's cocktail sauce, genius. Kind of defeats the purpose of having an oyster. An oyster is supposed to taste like eating the ocean. Like poetry in your mouth." Tobias ate his own oyster and then grabbed a shrimp and dipped it in the cocktail sauce. "Just try it. Be a man. You should have your man card revoked for coloring anyway."

I leaned over and whispered in Oliver's ear, "I bet watching you eat an oyster will make Dani extra horny for you."

A blush creeped up his face and the tips of his ears turned the color of the cocktail sauce. He looked over at Danica and then ate his oyster without another complaint. The table next to us clapped and I scowled at their intrusion. Oliver didn't seem to notice or he just didn't care.

He narrowed his eyes in contemplation and then grabbed another.

"What'd you say to him?" Danica asked, lifting her water and taking a drink.

"I told him that if you saw him suck down an oyster it would make you horny for him." I shrugged and took a bite of crab.

She turned her head to the side and started coughing as she choked on the water. Her eyes teared up. Tobias, who was next to her, patted her back. She continued to cough and splutter.

"Excuse me, I'm a mess," she barely managed to say. She stood and headed inside the restaurant.

"I should go make sure she's okay. After all we've been through, can't have her die choking on her damn water," I said before following her inside the noisy restaurant.

I turned the corner to the hall with the bathrooms and pushed the women's bathroom door open.

"Are you okay?" I asked, peeking my head inside. She was in an open stall and there was no one else inside.

I walked in and flipped the lock on the door. Women tended to freak out finding men in their bathrooms. Not that I had any experience with that. Nope, none at all.

I heard the toilet paper dispenser and she walked out of the stall wiping her eyes and nose.

"I swallowed wrong," she said clearing her throat several times.

I bit my lip, trying to hold back the comment I wanted to make. I had been binge watching too much of *The Office* and really wanted to say, "that's what she said."

She threw the toilet paper in the trash and then washed her hands, watching me in the mirror. She had a contemplative look on her face but said nothing as she turned around to face me.

"I just wanted to make sure you're okay. We're your guardians and all. Can you imagine us calling Lucifer and telling him you died from choking on ice water?"

"Is that why you followed me into the women's restroom and *locked* the door?" She closed the distance between us and put her hands on my chest. "My hero, saving me from the evil ice cubes."

I chuckled and put my hands over hers, moving them down to my growing erection. I had honestly followed her to check on her, but now that she brought it up, my dick was pretty happy to have her in a locked bathroom.

She stared back at me and raised her eyebrows as her hand began stroking me through my jeans. The bathroom wasn't the most appropriate place to get it on, but my dick didn't seem to care and neither did Danica.

Our lips met in a fevered kiss that left my brain feeling like mush. It was hard to put into words what kissing her was like. Whatever had been on my mind was forgotten and my sole focus was on her.

She deserved more than a quick bathroom fuck and I was about to pull away, but she was already unbuttoning my pants. We needed to be quick, but my brain wanted to kiss her for days.

I unbuttoned her pants and pulled them and her panties down past her ass. She insisted on wearing skin tight jeans so I moved her towards the sink and bent her over with her hands on the edge.

"Next time wear a dress or a skirt when we go out." I ran my hand over the smooth, milky skin of her ass and gave it a little pinch. Her breath hitched and she looked in the mirror and met my eyes.

"Next time don't follow me into the bathroom and my pants wouldn't be a problem." She cocked an eyebrow at me. She looked so damn sexy looking at me in the mirror, bent over, that I damn near came before I even got my dick out.

I pulled down my pants just enough so my cock sprung free. I put the tip against her ass, just to gauge her reaction. I hadn't broached the subject with her yet, but Toby and I had discussed it at length. She didn't need to know that though.

"I think we need some lube and foreplay for that." She bit her lip and reached her hand back to grip my cock.

I moved my dick to its intended destination and

pushed the tip in. Fuck, she was tight from not being able to spread her legs wide. On second thought, she should always wear tight jeans.

"And how would you know that?" I teased her pussy by barely pushing the tip in. I gritted my teeth and felt like my eyes wanted to roll back in my head.

"I've had anal a few times," she said with a shrug.

I thrust into her with a groan and bit down on the inside of my cheek. Her words alone were enough to make me come. I wanted to question her about her experiences with that, but our time was running out.

She gripped the edge of the counter as I increased my pace. The only sounds in the bathroom were our heated breaths, the smacking of our skin, and the bustling restaurant on the other side of the door.

I was so turned on and so into what we were doing, my brain just ignored the knocks on the door. I felt my orgasm creeping up on me. I slid my hand to Danica's clit, and worked it in quick strokes until her mouth opened in a quiet scream.

As her legs went weak and her body shook with release, I came inside her, her pussy milking every last drop from me.

I leaned into her to keep myself from falling over, because God damn that was good. Whatever worries had been on Danica's mind earlier, seemed to disappear.

"People keep knocking, we better get out of here before they start peeing themselves," she managed to say between breaths.

I pulled out of her and she went into a stall to clean herself up. I heard her zip up her pants and took that as my cue to leave the bathroom. Luckily no one was standing there as I exited. It was doubtful they would say anything anyways.

When I got back to the table, Tobias raised his eyebrows and then shook his head. I bet he wished he had been the one to follow her to the bathroom.

"Is Danica okay? You were gone an awfully long time," Oliver asked, seeming to have no clue what had just gone down.

"She's definitely okay, angel baby." I slapped him on the shoulder and then left my hand there for a few seconds longer than necessary.

I was pretty certain I was going to corrupt him.

Chapter Four

Danica

*G*roup dates needed to happen more often, and not just because of the impromptu bathroom sex Asher and I had. It was unexpected and quite the rush. Experiencing life like a normal person made me forget about everything else.

At least for that moment.

On the way back to Montecito, I let Tobias drive my car. Somehow, I managed to talk the angels into driving instead of flying. Olly insisted on sitting in the back with Asher, even though there wasn't much space for his legs. When I picked out my Nissan GTR, I never imagined I'd be cramming three full-sized men inside of it.

"Are we just going to go over to John's house and beat him up? Or should I text him and get him to meet us somewhere?" I asked as we drew closer to Montecito. My stomach was in knots thinking about seeing John again. If I had it my way, I'd never see him again.

"I don't think going to his house with three angels is a good idea. Maybe your old high school's parking lot? It'll be deserted," Asher suggested. I could hear him popping his knuckles in the back.

I turned and gave him a pointed look. "You aren't fighting so stop that."

"None of us should be fighting," Tobias warned as he merged onto the highway.

"How about this. You guys hold him and I'll throw the punches." It was a fair compromise. I had been the one beaten to shit by him; I should be the one to deliver the blows. Plus, I had no wings to lose.

I took my phone out and hesitated after pulling up John's contact information. Talking about kicking his ass was one thing, but actually doing it? I wasn't so sure if it was even worth it.

"What if he brings other people with him?" It was highly unlikely he'd just show up to meet me without backup. He wasn't an idiot.

"Then we kick all their asses," Asher replied and Olly agreed. I was surprised Olly was on board with the idea.

"Maybe this is a stupid idea." I closed out of the contact and put my phone in the cupholder.

So many things could go wrong. John could

recognize Asher and then would know I was involved in angel business. If he already knew, he did a good job of hiding it. I couldn't risk him finding out.

"It is," Tobias mumbled under his breath.

The last thing I needed was to look over my shoulder every time I was at home. If we beat up John, he would continue to come at me. Who knew what he was capable of since he was raised by a deranged doctor.

I turned and looked at Olly and Asher in the backseat. They both jerked their hands into their laps at the same time. I raised my eyebrows and smiled at them. They really weren't fooling anyone. We saw them touching all the time. It was subtle, but it was hard to miss. Plus, Olly looked at Asher the same way he looked at me.

"I appreciate that you two want to deliver justice, but if we beat him up, then he's going to come at me worse the next time I see him. This is a small suburb. I'll probably see him on occasion." I shuddered at the thought of always wondering when John would strike next.

Asher grunted and crossed his arms over his chest, but nodded in agreement.

"What are we going to do then? It's not even close to nine yet." Olly had a point; it was too early to go back to my house.

I looked over at Tobias. "Home Depot is still open."

"No. We aren't going to do that!" Tobias sounded like he was reaching his limit of bad ideas on my part. I couldn't help it. My mind was stuck on it. I had to know if everything was true.

I turned and looked at Asher and Olly again. "How do you feel about digging up my mother's grave?"

~

I SAT cross-legged on the damp grass watching three shirtless men as they shoveled dirt over the side of the hole they were in. Angels might not sweat, but apparently they got hot. Or maybe they just wanted to give me a show. I wasn't complaining in either case.

They were all covered in dirt thanks to Olly's inability to consistently get the dirt outside the three foot by seven-foot hole they were digging. They were only about four feet deep and they'd been digging for an hour.

Of course all of this would have been easier had we told my dad about it. He could have signed paperwork to exhume the body and they would have used a backhoe to get the casket out. Going down the legal route would take way too long though, and I had a feeling he wouldn't be onboard with us digging up the love of his life.

So naturally, instead, here we were in the darkness of night digging up my mother's grave.

Totally normal activities to pass the time.

I looked over at the black granite headstone.

Lily Judith Gardner

April 30, 1975 - January 20, 2001

Viva La Vida

On both sides of her name were Viva La Vida lilies. 'Long live life' was rather fitting considering my father was practically immortal. She might even be immortal too.

"I think I'm getting a side cramp. I knew those oysters were a bad idea," Olly moaned, snapping me out of my trance. I had been doing a lot of that lately, zoning out more than usual, my mind thinking of a million different scenarios. Not something I needed more of in my life.

"I'll give you a side cramp," Asher mumbled under his breath as he dug his shovel into the dirt and flung a pile out of the hole.

I laughed at their exchange and pulled my knees to my chest, resting my chin on my folded arms. How had I gotten so lucky to have three men in my life that would do anything for me? I thought I had lost them for good, but now that they were back I didn't plan on letting them go ever again.

Unless they wanted to go.

My head was still spinning from the information they came back from heaven with. All signs pointed to my mother being *the* Lilith. If her casket was empty, I would be ninety-five percent sure of it. The only true confirmation would have to come from the woman herself. If she were still alive, did I even want to meet her?

The fact that this was all part of some end of the world prophecy made things a little bleaker. At least that's what I *assumed* "saving the light from the dark" meant. Whoever decided it might be up to me, had to be on some serious crack.

"I don't think I was made for manual labor," Olly said, flopping down next to me and leaning back on his forearms. I hadn't even noticed he had climbed out.

"The hole wasn't big enough for three of us anyways." Tobias had his back to us but I could imagine him rolling his eyes.

"That's what she said." Asher laughed like it was the funniest thing in the world. I sincerely hoped he wasn't going to start saying that phrase all the time.

Olly sat up and put his arm around my waist, pulling me closer to him. I leaned back and tried to relax.

A lot was riding on this little field trip to the cemetery. The files were one thing, but verifying if she was in her grave was the real proof I needed. It would also mean my father was duped twenty years ago into falling in love and having me. I was pretty sure hell would implode if it were true.

Lucifer adored Lily. Her betrayal would most likely break him in a way I didn't want to be near him for.

"I'm worried about you Dani." Olly put his lips

to my temple. "I wish what I gave you was enough." He was referring to his ability to calm people's nerves with his touch. It worked for Asher, but not for me, at least not as much as I needed it to.

Before I was expelled from Montecito High and sent to the Angel Academy, I was blissfully unaware of what the true hardships in life were. All along I thought hardship was homework, suspensions and detentions, and a seldom seen father. Those were the hardships teenagers *should* have to face.

Now I felt the weight of the world on my shoulders and I didn't quite know what to do with that. I didn't even know what the weight of the world entailed just yet.

"We hit something," Tobias called out, his head the only thing visible. "Did you want us to look first?"

I nodded in response and then realized he couldn't see me. "Yeah." It was eerily silent besides the sounds of scraping and prying coming from the hole.

"Holy shit," Asher said. "Oliver, get her back to the house."

My heart seemed to stop for a few beats before beating wildly in my chest. I jumped up, but Olly grabbed me around the waist and started leading me towards my car. He had an unfair advantage of height, weight, and angel strength. He easily pulled me away.

"It's my mother's grave. I deserve to see whatever it is that's in there!" I yanked away from him when we got to the car, which was a short distance away.

Olly reached forward and I stepped back. I was acting unreasonable considering I didn't even know what was in the casket. They wouldn't have just sent me away unless it was serious, but at the same time it better be a damn bomb.

He ran his hand over his face and frowned back at me, an uncommon sight from him. He stepped forward and put his hands on either side of me against the car, trapping me.

"Sometimes we don't like what's best for us." I narrowed my eyes at his serious tone. "Sometimes what's best for us can end up changing our lives forever. Now let's do what Asher asked."

I looked up into his blue eyes which seemed a shade darker than their usual ocean blue color. I bit my lip and looked down at his lips, his bottom slightly bigger than the top, just begging to be kissed. Now wasn't the time or the place.

I pushed him away and opened the door, sliding into the driver's seat. Olly walked around and climbed in, sliding the seat back so he'd have more leg room. He hadn't asked to drive my car again; I think he was nervous after our run-in with a truck full of Fallen.

We rode to my house in silence. When we got inside he followed me upstairs to my room.

"How long do you think they're going to be

gone?" Olly asked, looking around my room and walking over to a large bookshelf. He picked up a few pictures on the shelf and examined them.

"Probably a while. They aren't just going to leave an open hole." I sat down on the edge of my bed and watched as he squatted down and pulled a box from the bottom shelf. "You sure are nosy. What if I have top secret love letters from past boyfriends in there?"

He shrugged. "Your past boyfriends have nothing on your current boyfriends. Did you save notes from your boyfriends?"

"Of course I did. They're in my closet some-where though. A well written note is something to be cherished. People just don't write each other notes anymore." It was true, I had saved every note ever passed between not only me and Ava, but anyone else too. It was fun to look back at them to see what ridiculous things they wrote.

"I know I've been in your room at school before, but that doesn't count. This is your actual room. The one you grew up in, right?" I nodded in response as he lifted the lid off the box and his face lit up. He emptied the box on the floor and grabbed a Ken doll.

How embarrassing.

"Just so we're clear, these are from when I was a kid." I sat on the floor next to him and grabbed a naked Barbie I had given a bad haircut to. "Poor

Jessica. No one told me the hair on these things didn't grow back."

"Jessica? They have names? Are you sure they're from when you were a kid? You still have them," he teased.

"It's hard to get rid of something you spent a lot of time playing with. And yes, I named them all. You are holding Jessica's super rich, trust fund boyfriend, Trent. He likes long walks on the beach, working out, and kissing Jessica under the stars."

He raised an eyebrow, his eyes twinkling in amusement, and looked at me. "Kissing? That's it? With these abs, you'd think she'd be in his pants." He slid the board shorts that were on the doll off and laughed. "Although he doesn't have much to work with."

"I remember the first time I saw a penis, I freaked out. I thought everyone had vaginas because Trent looked just like Jessica. They still had the Barbie equivalent of sex though. Face smashing." I grabbed his doll and smashed his face into the Barbie. If they were real people there would have been lost teeth and bruised faces. Maybe a concussion or brain bleed too. "Trent really knew how to give it to her."

Olly laughed and laid back on the carpet, lacing his fingers behind his head. "I feel like I missed out on pivotal developmental things, like toys and coloring. Going to school. Other things. Instead I just woke up one day."

I set the dolls down and swiveled towards him. "I think that makes you intriguing. I know we poke fun at you a lot, but I hope you know it's because we love you."

"I know that. I just feel like I have all this knowledge about my world, but when it comes to this one, I'm an idiot. I'm a virgin in every sense of the word." He was avoiding my eyes, a faint blush blooming on his freckled cheeks.

"You aren't an idiot and there's nothing wrong with being a virgin." There was a long silence and my mind started to wander back to the cemetery.

"Do you want to have sex?" He cleared his throat. "With me?"

Him asking was a shocker. I thought it would just kind of happen one day. I did want to have sex with him, every time I saw him. Despite having frequent sex with Asher and Tobias both separate and together, Olly was the missing piece of the puzzle. We had waited long enough.

Originally I hadn't made any moves because a small part of me didn't trust him. But now, it was hard not to trust him with every fiber of my being. If he happened to be playing a long game of deceit for the Divine then I'd cut off his dick.

With a butter knife.

Making out and dry humping each other was driving me mad. I wanted to be respectful of him and his need to "research enough so I know what I'm doing" (his words, not mine), but being left in a constant state of arousal by him was frustrating. I was glad we were finally on the same page.

I crawled over to him and sat on his thighs. I was more than ready after the little sex-capade with Asher.

He sat up and looked at me with a serious expression before placing his hands on my thighs and capturing my lips with his. It was the type of kiss that made me want to live attached to his mouth. Sweet and gentle.

That was short-lived though. He grabbed my hips as he pulled my bottom lip between his. His mouth began working against mine in a rush of hormones and need. I could feel his hard length straining against his pants.

"This is really happening," he whispered as his mouth slid to the sensitive skin below my ear. It was my favorite spot to be kissed and all three of them knew it opened up my floodgates. I moaned and grinded my hips against him.

His hands slid under my shirt and I grabbed the hem and pulled it over my head. He reached behind me, unclasping my bra before ripping it off and flinging it across the room. He pushed me back a little on his thighs and stared down at my exposed breasts.

This was only the second time he had been up close and personal with them, and this time he was sober. The last time was months ago after we made the poor decision to play Never Have I Ever. Since then he had only seen them if he was watching me with the others. Which had only been a few times.

"You're perfect." He slid his thumbs over my nipples and pulled me back towards him, lowering his mouth and biting one gently.

"Oliver," I breathed, my eyes closing and my fingers gripping onto his hair. We had months of foreplay leading up to this moment, which made every touch of his hands or lips that much more potent.

I just hoped that if Asher and Tobias came back in the middle of this distraction from real life, that they wouldn't interrupt us from our moment together. This was his moment.

I fumbled to get his pants undone and my fingertips connected with the head of his cock.

"Fuck, that feels so good," he mumbled around my nipple. I let out a breathy laugh at his sudden use of the word fuck. We needed to start a swear jar for Asher; he was a bad influence.

Olly grabbed the back of my legs and stood up with me wrapped around his middle. He walked towards the bed, setting me down. He took off his shirt and slid his pants and boxers down as he kicked off his shoes.

"How is your cock just as beautiful as you are?" I gripped him at his base and pumped him a few times before he pushed me back on the bed and took off my jeans.

He kissed his way down my stomach, occasionally scraping his teeth across the skin. His hands slid under the waistband of my panties and pulled them off. All I really wanted was for him to be inside of me, where I had been yearning for him for so long. I trusted him completely. He may have been a teensy bit of an asshole when we first met, but he had more than redeemed himself.

He was about to redeem himself even more by putting his mouth between my legs.

He planted kisses on my thighs and along my slit before his tongue dipped into the wet heat begging to be tasted. I arched into him and let out a satisfied sigh. He licked the length of me from bottom to top before swirling his tongue over my clit.

I threaded my fingers in his hair as he brought me closer and closer to an orgasm. I gripped my comforter as he slid two fingers into me and began pumping them at the same pace as the flick of his tongue. *Good lord.* How was he so good at this already?

My climax crashed into me with such force that my ears rang and there was a rush of wet heat between my legs. I pushed at Olly's head before he killed me and managed to push him on his back to straddle him, his dick nestled in my folds.

I cupped his cheek. "Are you sure you're ready for this? It's a big step."

"This is perfect. You're perfect." He turned his head and kissed my palm.

I leaned forward and kissed him gently as I lined him up with my opening and slowly lowered onto his length. He let out all the air in his lungs with a groan. In one swift movement, he flipped us and nestled himself between my legs.

He moved with long, slow strokes that left me yearning for more. How we had managed to wait this long was still baffling to me. It sure had taken every ounce of *my* willpower not to throw myself at him every chance I got.

He buried his face in the crook of my neck as his thrusts gradually increased in urgency. I dug my nails into his shoulder blades where his wings usually appeared.

He growled deep in his throat. "Again."

I felt another orgasm building at the sounds of his grunts and growls. The sounds were so primal coming from him. I arched my back, my clit rubbing against his pelvis every time he thrust.

"Oh, Oliver." I dug my nails into him as my orgasm hit me hard, my pussy clenching around him.

He gave one last thrust, spilling himself inside of me. His lips brushed over mine as he came down from his high.

"I love you." He put his forehead against my sweaty one.

"I love you too." I ran my fingers up and down his spine.

Once he'd regained his breath, he rolled off of

me and pulled me towards him, tucking me into his side. I put my hand on his chest and threw a leg over his thigh.

"That was amazing. Are you doing okay?" I lightly patted his chest.

"Yes. That was better than chocolate chip cookies if I'm being honest."

I let out a half moan, half laugh. "Nice to know how I rank against cookies."

After a few more minutes of recovery, Olly put his hand over mine. "Would you tell me if it was bad?"

What kind of question was that? I'd clearly had two orgasms, which was a testament to whatever research he had performed. Maybe he had a blow-up sex doll for practice. I wouldn't have been surprised.

I propped myself up on my elbow and looked down at him. "I would. You aren't though. It's only going to get even more amazing."

We heard footsteps on the stairs but didn't move. A rap of knuckles knocked on the door and then the door slowly opened. Both Tobias and Asher stopped in their tracks when they saw Olly and I buck naked on top of the covers. Neither of us moved to cover up, although after finding my dad in my room after a shower, I probably should have been more concerned at who was at my bedroom door.

"It's about damn time," Asher said, a grin spreading across his dirt-smeared face.

I rolled my eyes and got up from the bed. I felt their eyes watching me as I walked into the bathroom and shut the door. I was still trying to figure out how having three boyfriends was supposed to work. Would one of them get jealous one of these days and just leave?

I cleaned up and walked back into the room, finding all three men lounging on my bed. Olly had put his pants back on. Their eyes were on me again as I purposely swung my hips a little more than usual and bent over to grab my clothes off the floor.

"That ass deserves an award," Tobias murmured. "Hurry up and put some clothes on before I come over there and have my turn with it."

After pulling on my clothes, I joined them on the bed, letting Tobias pull me into his lap. He still had dirt on him, but I wasn't about to complain.

"What was in the grave?" I asked, turning so I could look at Tobias. I usually deferred my questions to him because he was most likely to know the answers. Plus, he was kind of the leader of our group. I wouldn't be caught dead telling him that though.

I fiddled with my hands, nervous about what his answer would be. I had a sickening feeling in my stomach. Olly had distracted me for a while, but now the unease was back.

Asher looked at Tobias in some kind of silent

communication. It seemed they were deciding who was going to tell me what they had found. Their silence spoke volumes.

"Was it empty or was she in it?" I sighed and ran my hand through my hair. Where had my hair tie gone?

"The grave was empty except for a symbol painted with blood. At least we think it was blood." Asher handed over his cell phone that had a picture pulled up. I took it gingerly in my hands as if it might break. I frowned at the image of the letter C.

"Why a C? What does it mean?" I handed the phone to Olly. His eyes widened and he zoomed in and then back out.

"It's not a C, it's a crescent moon. There are many rumors and beliefs here on Earth about the origins and location of Lilith. Almost all of them in some way incorporate the night or darkness. A crescent moon is a common symbol that humans use for her. Interesting she would choose to use it like that," Olly said. He looked over at me and handed the phone back to Asher. "But she can't be Lilith. You're half human. Besides, a demon and an archangel having a baby? I don't think so."

My eyes widened and I looked down at my lap. They thought I was half human because that's what my father and I always thought. Now, it seemed I wasn't. I should tell them about the medical files, but I was scared of what they might say or do. I wasn't sure they'd take well to knowing they'd been fucking a demon.

"What is it Dani?" Asher asked softly.

"Nothing, just a lot to process. I don't think we'll ever know the whole story unless we actually talk to her. It's probably not safe though, considering she's also most likely behind whatever was planned with the angel blood." I finally looked up and met his eyes. He didn't look worried often, but a small crease had appeared between his brows.

"What was in the medical files you stole?" *Crap.* I never had told them what was in the files, just that I had stolen them.

I looked back down again and silence filled the room for several awkward minutes. They were waiting for me to talk. What if I never talked? Would we sit there in silence for eternity?

"Danica." Tobias squeezed my hip and put his chin on my shoulder. "We're in this together. No secrets."

I sighed and cleared my throat, as if that would give me some magical ability to find my voice. "My dad is obviously an angel. My blood work was inconclusive."

I shut my eyes briefly and opened them, hoping by chance that we'd moved on from our conversation and the next question would never come.

"And your mother?" Tobias asked gently, his thumb moving reassuringly back and forth across my hip.

"There was only her autopsy results."

"You're not telling us everything." Asher looked straight at me, frowning.

Yeah, I was omitting some facts.

"Everything pointed to her being human. Whether or not that was a fabrication, well, we'd have to find Dr. Adamson and ask." I snapped my mouth shut and wiggled out of Tobias's lap, causing him to grunt as my ass hit his dick. "I'm tired. Can we just go to sleep?"

No one argued with me, thankfully sensing that the conversation was over and I wasn't going to say more. I just wasn't ready to let that tiny piece of information out into the world yet.

Chapter Five

I wasn't supposed to have any nightmares with Asher around. I had gone to sleep feeling relief that he was around, sleeping on an air mattress with Olly in my bedroom. As soon as I woke, my hair plastered to my head with sweat, my heart beating wildly, I knew that it wasn't Asher keeping the nightmares away.

It was something else.

I just wasn't ready to admit it to myself yet.

I stared up at the ceiling; something that seemed to be becoming a new hobby of mine. The deep sounds of breathing filled my ears and taunted me.

I rolled over. Faint light coming through the curtains. The sun was just starting to rise and I could hear a few birds starting their incessant chattering in the nearby trees.

I wiggled out of Tobias's arms and slipped into the bathroom to wash my face and brush my teeth.

I felt dirty, like I was somehow tainted by the knowledge that my mother might have faked her own death. Why would she do something like that to her own flesh and blood? To someone who had loved her with all his heart?

I pulled on my robe and headed downstairs to the smell of bacon frying. I got to the bottom of the stairs. My father was in the kitchen cooking. It was an odd sight, seeing him preparing breakfast in jeans and a t-shirt.

He cursed as a piece of bacon popped. I laughed at his reaction and slid onto a barstool at the island.

"Good morning." He turned and looked at me, the smile he wore not reaching his eyes. He looked like he hadn't slept well. Something we had in common. "I see Oliver was able to heal you. Sorry I rushed out of here like that."

He turned back to the stove and I reached across the counter to grab a glass and the carton of orange juice sitting out. I was almost tempted to drink coffee to wake myself up, but even the smell made me want to vomit.

"Yeah, about that. Why did you rush out of here?" I took a sip and scrunched my face having taken a drink too soon after brushing my teeth.

He turned around again and let out a chuckle. "You would think by now you'd learn not to do that."

I shrugged in response. I never remembered

until it was too late. He walked over to the refrigerator and got out a bottle of water to hand to me.

"I left so abruptly because when you told me about Ava, I knew exactly who had caused it. You remember that night I called you two girls prostitutes?"

I snorted. Of course I remembered that night. Who could forget the moment their dad acted like his daughter and her best friend were working girls and sent them back up to his room? It had all been a cover to keep the demon that had been in the kitchen from knowing I was his daughter.

"Well, that *was* one of my most trusted demons that I leave in charge when I'm not there. He took his new liberties the job gave him, to come here and torment people. Ava caught his eye." He shook his head and ran a hand through his hair. I noticed he wasn't wearing one of his fancy watches today.

"What about Ava? Is she in danger?" I took a steadying breath. It seemed everything I touched was in danger these days.

"Not anymore, I kicked him out of my territory in hell and took away his ability to come here. I will have one of my lawyers look into her case." He put the tongs he had been flipping bacon with down and turned to look at me.

I nodded and played with the water bottle cap on the counter.

"What's on your mind? Besides Ava," he said, breaking the silence that had settled around us.

"She really was Lilith wasn't she?" I didn't look up, fearing what his answer would be.

Several long moments passed. He cleared his throat and I looked up, meeting his stormy eyes. The intelligence in them always amazed me and also unnerved me. He had lived a long time. Would I live just as long?

"Michael is having some of his soldiers look for John to get answers. He seems to have dropped off the radar. We think the woman behind all of this is Lilith. We just can't rely on a prophecy to identify your mother." He ran a hand over his face and then through his hair. He had been doing that a lot. I never knew he had a nervous tick.

"Dad, I need to tell you something. Last night we-"

Olly appeared in the kitchen, somehow getting down the stairs and several feet into the room without being heard. I snapped my mouth shut, not wanting to discuss the potential of me being some demon-angel hybrid freak in front of the others.

It always amazed me how the largest of the three angels could appear in a room so quietly. He was so stealthy he put all superheroes to shame. And right now he was standing in only his boxers, sporting morning wood in front of my father.

"Morning." He was rubbing his eyes as he made his way to the refrigerator and stood with the door open, staring inside. He didn't seem to process the fact that the man in the kitchen was Lucifer. Maybe it was because he was dressed so casually he was unrecognizable.

My dad made a coughing noise and Olly shut the door slowly. He still looked half asleep.

"Son, you need to go upstairs and put some clothes on. Now." He raised his eyebrows and then looked down at Olly's crotch.

I couldn't help but laugh as Olly finally zeroed in on my father and his eyes widened. Now he was awake.

He left as quickly as he had arrived and my dad cracked a smile. "Why is he so easy to torment? Maybe he wasn't created for you, but for me to torment the hell out of." As if realizing what he just said, he closed his mouth and his jaw ticked.

"Created for me?" I put my chin on my fists.

He looked thoughtful for a few moments before opening his mouth again. "I think the more appropriate explanation is he was sent to you. You know how each archangel has a purpose? " I nodded. "Well, his purpose is to act as a balance."

"A balance of what?" I furrowed my brows.

"Light and dark, good and evil, love and hate. That's why he is so even in temperament."

I considered his words. "So him being an asshole when I first met him was a balance?"

"He's not perfect. All angels have a learning curve." He laughed and took a tray of biscuits out of the oven. "His just took an interesting turn."

"Since when do you cook?" The buttery scent hit my nose and my mouth watered.

"I've always been able to cook, I just haven't had the desire." He turned off all the burners on the stove. "Go get all of your boyfriends up. The food is ready."

It still amazed me that he was fine with me having more than one boyfriend. He hadn't even batted an eyelid. He had seen and heard it all apparently.

After waking up Tobias and Asher, and convincing Olly that my dad wasn't going to kill him for having a boner in the kitchen, we gathered around the dining room table. Everyone was impressed by the biscuits and gravy and the perfectly cooked bacon that was crispy but not burnt.

"What did you four do last night? Danica was about to tell me when Woody wandered into the kitchen." My dad put his fork down on his empty plate and leaned back in his chair.

Olly's cheeks turned pink and I suppressed a laugh. My dad had made it his mission to give Olly as much shit as possible and he didn't need any more ammo. He never teased or tormented Asher and Tobias.

They all looked at me, waiting for me to answer the question. I didn't think the breakfast table, where we were all still in our pajamas, was the place to tell Lucifer that we had dug up his love's grave because I was a neurotic mess.

"Danica." The warning in his voice was clear. It was that tone parents got when they knew you were hiding something and they wanted the truth, or *else*.

"Why don't you guys go upstairs and change?" I was pretty sure that my dad was going to have a less than favorable reaction to what we did last night and didn't want them to bear any of the fallout.

"What did you do?" He narrowed his eyes at me and I felt hot. How the hell did he do that? It was like he had turned up my internal thermostat a few degrees.

Tobias, Asher, and Olly stood to leave.

"Sit."

Their asses hit their chairs and they kept their eyes averted from us. They looked like scolded puppies who had been caught tearing up the house. All they needed were the shame signs.

"Dad, I don't think... let's talk alone." I stood and gave him a pleading look. I didn't know how he was going to react.

"If they were with you, then they are just as responsible. And my guess is from how all four of you are acting, that it wasn't something good." His voice was neutral, which was the scariest of all because that meant he was holding back his emotions.

I put my hands on the edge of the table and braced myself. I should have considered this last night, but I also had been hopefully optimistic that the casket wouldn't be empty and we would just pretend it never happened.

For once in my life, I went over my words in my head. I needed all the blame to fall on me, not the others.

"I made them dig up Mom's grave. It was empty and had a crescent symbol drawn in blood."

My heart was beating so hard I was certain it was about to stop working from overuse. Hearing my own words come from my mouth, made me feel sick. *We dug up a grave last night.*

The silence was deafening. My dad's jaw ticked and then he stood abruptly. I gripped the table, my knuckles turning white.

"Get out."

"What?" My voice was shaking. What did he mean, get out? Was he talking to me?

"Get. Out," he repeated, his words coming out between his clenched teeth.

I stared at him, not completely comprehending his words. I felt a hand on my arm and was led out of the dining room and upstairs. My bedroom door wasn't even shut all the way when we heard a large crash from downstairs.

WE SAT on the roof in a tight circle around the

unlit fire pit. My cheeks were stained from tears. I had fucked up royally this time.

Once the noise from downstairs had stopped, we had taken our bags and gone downstairs. My dad was gone, but the dining room and living room were trashed. The table was flipped, the television was cracked with a broken lamp laying under it, and glass was everywhere. There were even singe marks marring the couch and chairs. I hadn't even known my dad was capable of producing flames.

No one had said a word. Instead, Tobias drove me back in my car, while Asher and Olly stayed to clean up a bit before flying back to Asher's place.

"He hates me." It had been hours since any of us had spoken. My voice sounded foreign to my ears.

"He doesn't hate you. He's hurt. I don't think it had anything to do with you." I was surprised at Olly's insight. "You just told him that the woman he loved was not who he thought she was."

I looked down at my nails that were almost bitten down to the quick. I never bit my nails. Until today. I frowned down at them. Wasn't I doing the same thing to them as my mother had done to my father?

"He's your father, he could never hate you. Give him some time." Tobias ran his hand over his beard and then reached for my hand. I let him take it and he ran his thumb over the ends of my fingers.

The rooftop went silent again, the only sound

the noise from the street below. It was overcast, the sun hidden behind a blanket of clouds. It was fitting considering the mood.

"We should do something to take our minds off things," Olly suggested.

I looked up at him and examined his face and demeanor. Now that I knew more about him, I was going to pay closer attention. He was the least affected by what had happened. His body was relaxed and his face was content.

"Now is not the time for sex, angel baby. I know that now you popped your cherry you're going to want it all the time, but now is not that time." Asher had his chin in his hand and he looked over at Olly as he spoke.

Olly just smiled in response and then turned his attention to me. "Let's go do something."

"What did you have in mind?" I pulled out my phone and opened the document I had started listing all the things Olly hadn't experienced. It was fairly long and I started listing off all that was on the list.

"Universal Studios!" His eyes lit up and he moved to the edge of his seat. "That will cheer us right up."

"I'm not sure I'm up for faking a good time." I put my phone away and Olly's face fell. "You guys can go."

"I know you probably don't want to hear any advice right now, but keeping busy will help you keep your mind off of it. There's no point in sitting here and marinating in your unhappiness. Trust me on that." Asher stood and stretched his arms over his head. My eyes fell on the sliver of stomach showing as his shirt lifted. So did Olly's.

I sighed and squinted up at him, the day still bright despite the overcast skies. "Are *you* going to be all right going to a place like that?"

He shrugged his shoulders and looked at Olly. "I think I'll be fine."

I'LL ADMIT IT. I was having fun, especially after my dad texted me back after I sent numerous apology texts. He said he was fine and we'd talk later. I tried to push the negative thoughts that had been running through my head away for the time being.

We walked through the gates of Hogwarts School of Witchcraft and Wizardry, and made our way along the path. I felt like I was walking up to Hogwarts itself.

We walked through a stone archway and into a dark and damp tunnel. Asher and Olly walked in front and Asher stepped closer to Olly, their arms connecting as they walked.

Once we were back outside again under the frosted glass of the greenhouse, Asher's shoulders relaxed. I had been worried about him coming to a theme park because the sheer amount of people and the noises were overwhelming at times. Whatever Olly was doing, seemed to be keeping him, well, balanced.

We walked back inside after the winding pathway ended and into the halls of Hogwarts. Tobias and I followed Asher and Olly, who were chatting animatedly.

"What do you think is going on with them?" Tobias said in my ear so they wouldn't hear.

"Something special." I didn't quite know how to respond to his question. There were moments between them that transcended the boundaries between friends and more than friends.

Although, I guess that would be the case in a relationship like we had. Tobias wasn't like that with either of them though. He was closest to Asher, but they didn't walk around touching arms or hold hands secretly. At least, not that I had seen.

After the ride, we exited back outside and made our way towards the bathrooms. It had taken almost an hour for the ride and before that we had all drank butterbeers.

I stood in the line for the women's restroom. Someone tapped on my shoulder and I turned. The woman looked familiar, but I couldn't quite place her. Her hair was pulled back through a baseball cap. Half her face was covered in a large pair of sunglasses.

"Can I help you?" I turned my body to the side so I could still watch the line moving in front of me.

"I couldn't help but notice outside that you are with three very gorgeous men." Her voice was seductive and I felt myself leaning towards her slightly, drawn into the sound.

"I am." I wasn't sure what else to say. I didn't know if this woman was about to compliment me for having three boyfriends or give me her opinion about how wrong it was.

"You're with them all? Romantically?" Her voice sounded curious but I narrowed my eyes anyway. She noticed and held up a hand. "There's nothing wrong with it, I was just wondering."

I looked past her and outside but couldn't see the men in question anywhere. I looked back at the woman and looked at where her eyes were. I hated not seeing people's eyes.

"We are, yes." She smiled broadly at my response and then tapped her bottom lip with her pristinely manicured nail.

"My daughter is in a similar relationship, but with four men. Do you have more or just the three?"

I felt myself flush. Four boyfriends? How would I handle that? This woman had some balls talking to me about my relationship.

"Nope, just the three." I turned back around and moved forward in line. I was almost at the front.

I turned back to tell the woman she should consider minding her own business in the future but she was gone. The woman now behind me raised her eyebrows at my confused face and took hold of her little girl's hand.

"What happened to the woman that was right behind me?"

"What? I've been behind you the entire time." The woman backed up a step.

"I was talking to a woman, she had on a baseball cap, big glasses." I knew I was freaking the woman out, especially because she had her little girl with her.

"You haven't said anything until just now when you turned around. It's your turn."

I turned back around and walked to the open stall.

What the hell had just happened?

Chapter Six

Reve

*W*atching them together was killing me. For weeks I had endured these men that kept her from me. I hadn't seen Danica in days. It was the weekend, when she was typically at Asher's, but this weekend she was gone and so was Asher.

I sat in the dark room, waiting. I felt like a damn stalker.

In a way, I suppose I was.

It was a Sunday and there were unpacked bags in the living room. Wherever they had gone, they were back, just not here. The weekends were the only times she was here and the only time she was accessible to me.

I had followed her on my bike one evening and most of the time she was hidden away at some kind of angel military fortress. I couldn't even get within ten feet of the boundary without feeling intense pain.

This never should have happened, me falling for a woman inside of her dreams. I needed her more than she needed me. She had woken me up from my own nightmare that I lived day after day, night after night.

After my first night with her, I had tried to replicate what had happened with her, with others. It never worked and my hunger for fear would overwhelm me. I could only produce nightmares with everyone except her.

The door to the roof opened and the four I had become way too familiar with came down the stairs. They had flown wherever they had disappeared to. I watched as they sat down around the kitchen table, a pizza box placed in the middle.

I moved to the kitchen and hopped up on the countertop to be closer. No one looked in my direction. They were talking about a flood, an earthquake, and a shark.

"I wish I had recorded him screaming when that shark came out of the water. It was so plastic-looking and fake that I'm actually surprised I was the one that had to calm *you* down." Asher laughed as Oliver narrowed his eyes at him.

I watched them as they finished eating and chatted. They all seemed to be in great moods, except for Danica. She did have a smile on her face, but something was wrong. It was a fake smile.

She kept taking her hair out of her ponytail, running her fingers through it, and putting it back up. It took everything in me not to waltz over to her and bury my face in the soft strands. It was probably just as I had imagined it, soft and silky.

Tobias reached over and took her hand. He must have noticed her mood before the other two. The other two had increasingly become more and more infatuated with each other over the last several weeks. It was subtle when they were around Danica and Tobias, but I was certain they held flames for each other.

Jealousy surged in me as Tobias stood and wrapped his arms around Danica from behind. They all touched her entirely too much for my liking and I considered ripping their throats out while they slept on a nightly basis.

Weren't they supposed to be angels? What they did to her on the regular was not very holy at all. The only thing holy about them was that they stuck their dicks in her holes.

If anyone should have been shoving things inside her, it was me.

"What am I going to do if Lilith really is my mother?" she asked out of nowhere. "We need to find her. I need to know for sure."

I hopped off the counter and paced the length of the kitchen. It couldn't be that they were looking for Lilith, could it? The rumor was she disappeared from Inferna decades ago and hadn't been seen since. Thank fuck for that.

I shuddered at the thought of the woman who had caused me and my family so much pain. She needed to be put down. If that was even remotely possible.

"I don't think that's a good idea considering she likes to drain angels of their blood," Tobias said, his chin resting on the top of her head.

It was no secret that Lilith had a few screws loose. The entire demon population of Inferna had suffered at her hands. Many of us, including me, escaped her rule centuries ago and swore fealty to Lucifer. Some disappeared into the vast emptiness beyond the cities or remained loyal to her crazy delusions of grandeur.

If Lilith really was here on Earth, Earth was screwed.

"Excuse me." Danica stood and walked towards the bathroom. Oliver stood to follow her but Asher grabbed his arm, stopping him.

The bathroom door slid shut behind her and I heard the lock slide into place. I frowned at the three men around the table. Here they were making her suffer again. Her suffering should have fueled me; instead it seemed to drain me. This should be enough to make me stay far away, but I was a glutton for punishment, even if it was my own.

"I think we need to consider telling Michael to

fuck off about this whole prophecy thing. She's still dealing with everything that's happened. It's too soon to expect her to handle all of this well." Asher stood and walked past me to pour himself a glass of whiskey.

It figured the drunken tormented one was the one with any sense. I would have given anything to get in his dreams and feast on his pain. Too bad I couldn't access angel brains.

"You know we can't do that. We need to talk to Lucifer about this once he's calmed down and find out more about Lilith. If Michael is right about this prophecy then Danica is the key to saving us all," Tobias said, raising his eyebrows as he watched Asher drink the entire glass of whiskey.

"The prophecy said 'save the light from the dark' not the end of the world. Besides, the prophecy might not even be about her, there are only three of us." Olly put his chin in his hand and watched as Asher poured another glass.

"The other guardian could be her father. It didn't say all of her guardians needed to be in a relationship with her." Asher returned to the table and sat down. "Michael seems to think it is about us though."

"You could be right, Lucifer has been around more lately," Tobias said.

My stomach dropped and I almost lost control of my phantom form. Lucifer was her father. *Crap.* I unconsciously put my hands over my crotch. He would lop off my balls if he knew what I was doing in her dreams.

My attention went to the bathroom door, where I could hear her crying on the other side. I made my way to the door and walked through it, finding her sitting on the floor against the cabinets. She had her knees drawn up and her face buried in her arms.

I wanted to give her comfort but couldn't until she fell asleep. I sat on the floor across from her, leaning against the clear glass of the shower. Would it be so bad if I revealed myself to her? Would she run away screaming knowing I was the one she dreamed about?

She looked up and right at where I was sitting. I knew she couldn't see me, but it didn't stop my heart from spluttering in my chest.

A soft knock came at the door, snapping us both out of our stare off. If it could be called that.

"Dani, are you okay?" Tobias asked, concern in his voice.

"Yeah. I'll be out in a second." She stood and splashed her face with cold water before exiting the bathroom.

They were getting ready for bed finally. Asher went to the couch and Oliver and Tobias sandwiched Danica in between them in the bed. It was an interesting setup they had going.

As soon as Tobias and Danica were asleep, Oliver slid from the bed and made his way to the couch. He had done this every time they all slept over on the weekends. He would slip out of bed after the other two were asleep and then slip back in before they woke.

Oliver and Asher were much *friendlier* with each other now. Tonight they were practically intertwined facing each other. Asher was always stiff at first before relaxing and drifting off to sleep, usually while Oliver stroked his hair or back. I wondered what Danica would think of their secret night time couch rendezvous?

I made my way to the bed and hovered just over it. Tobias was behind her, wrapped around her in his typical protective manner. He couldn't protect her from me though, no one could.

I shut my eyes and pushed into her dream.

BLACKNESS ENGULFED her as she stood over four rectangular holes in the ground. She stood unmoving, except for her eyes which landed on each of the four headstones at the top of the graves.

Tobias Armstrong.

Asher Thorne.

Oliver Morgan.

The Fourth.

I approached and stood by her side, taking her hand in mine. The holes were empty. She looked over at me and then back at the empty graves, except now they weren't empty. Each of the men stared blankly up at the black sky.

Danica let go of my hand and a shovel appeared. She began shoveling dirt into each of the graves, burying the bodies. The last hole held a faceless body.

I grabbed her hand and pulled her away.

"Where are we going?" she asked, sadness seeping out of her voice. Her dream tonight was a new one. Typically she dreamed of Asher's death or her imprisonment.

"Have you ever been to Capri, Italy?" I flashed her my award-winning smile before the landscape around us changed and we were on a terrace at La Terrazza di Lucullo restaurant at the Caesar Augustus Hotel, overlooking the Bay of Naples.

She needed more tonight and I was pulling out all the stops.

She gasped and rushed to the railing as she took in the sunset that made the water appear purple. I joined her and put my arm around her, resting my hand on her hip.

"Do you like it? We can go somewhere else if it's not to your liking."

She shook her head and turned her head to look up at me. "You're crazy. It's perfect."

I took her hand and led her to the single table on the terrace. Several candles were lit and a champagne bucket sat with ice and a bottle of vintage Dom Perignon.

I poured her a glass and sat back in my chair, watching as she took a sip and scrunched up her nose. Every time I gave her champagne she'd do the same.

"What's your name?" she asked as she took a bite of our seared tuna appetizer. Food wasn't necessary, but was something she enjoyed.

"You know I can't tell you that."

She asked me in every dream, and every time my answer was the same. I was already breaking all the rules by showing her my face.

"Not even a hint?" She set her fork down and put her hand on my wrist, tracing the edge of my tattoo peeking out of my shirt.

I watched as her index finger traced the inked chain links circling my wrist. The same chain that was tattooed around my other wrist, my ankles, and the base of my neck. I shut my eyes and cleared my throat, her touch sending a foreign sensation up my arm.

"It's French in origin, but I'm not from France." I opened my eyes and she was staring back at me, a small smile on her lips.

"Then where are you from?" She threaded her fingers through mine and brought them to her lips, placing a kiss on my fingers. Why was she so perfect?

"Here and there." I stood and grabbed the bottle of champagne and my glass. "Let's go."

She grabbed her own glass and I changed the

scene to inside a cliff-side suite overlooking the bay. I hadn't brought her to a room yet, but tonight I felt bold. I wanted her, even if it was just in a dream.

She glanced around the room, taking in the canopy bed and the views before turning towards me. "Are you seducing me, Frenchie?"

Her nickname sent shivers down my spine. "Depends. Are you seducible?"

She drank the rest of her champagne before spotting the rose petals on the floor and narrowing her eyes at me.

"I am if you tell me your name."

Giving her some freedoms in these dreams was blowing up in my face. Her knowing my name would put me at risk of Lucifer finding out about this. Dream demons did not duplicate names and if she happened to say it in conversation, he'd know.

Trying to distract her from my name, I grabbed her hand and led her to the bathroom that had a jacuzzi tub filled with bubbles. It was surrounded by candles and rose petals.

"Let me bathe you." I took her glass and set it on the side of the tub with mine and the bottle of champagne.

I began unbuttoning my shirt as she watched, licking her lips as it fell open, revealing my heavily tattooed torso. My blue dress shirt fell to the ground and I unhooked my belt, smiling as she took a loud inhale of breath as I pulled it out of the loops and it dropped with a clink to the marble floor.

I popped the button on my slacks and slowly pulled down the zipper, keeping my eyes locked on hers. Her eyes widened and then darkened in anticipation as I pushed my slacks and boxers down slightly, stopping at the base of my dick. It was already hardening as her eyes perused my body.

I pushed them down the rest of the way and stepped out of them, kicking them to the side and standing in front of her in all my glory. She took in a deep breath and then turned around, pulling her hair to the side so I could unzip her dress.

She shivered as I took my time sliding the zipper down and then lowered the thin spaghetti straps down her shoulders. She wasn't wearing a bra or panties, so as soon as her dress slid off her body I was treated with a view that was better than anything Italy had to offer.

"You're exquisite," I whispered into her neck. "The most beautiful woman I've had the pleasure of laying my eyes on."

Goosebumps spread across her skin and I ran my hands up and down her arms. She turned and I scanned her body, taking in her full breasts that would fit perfectly in my hands, the slight flair of her hips that were perfect for grabbing onto, and her delicious looking pussy. It was going to be difficult to control myself tonight.

Taking her hand, I helped her into the tub before joining her and pulling her to rest against my chest. I knew she could feel how hard I was, my erection was pressed up against her lower back.

"Do you not trust me?"

And there it was, we were back to my name.

I grabbed a washcloth and dipped it into the water before I ran it along her upper back. I didn't speak, hoping she would lose her mind and just stick to calling me Frenchie. I could live with that.

She sighed as I moved my hands around to her front, starting with her stomach, before moving up to her breasts. I took my time rubbing the cloth over her erect nipples. I dropped the cloth and took both her breasts in my hands, massaging them gently.

"Whose name am I supposed to moan?" She scooted up against me and wiggled her ass into my erection, causing me to groan. "Whose name am I supposed to scream when I come?"

I ran my lips along her shoulder and placed them under her ear, sucking the skin and then taking her earlobe between my teeth. I pinched her nipples and she let out a whimper.

My resolve to keep my name from her was thinning quickly, as she covered my hands with hers and then moved one of them down her body to her clit. I rubbed the sensitive nub between my fingers, drawing shaky breaths from her.

"Please."

I buried my face in her neck and willed myself not to speak as she began undulating her hips against my hand, the water starting to slosh against the sides of the tub. I moved my hand further down and slid a finger inside of her tight heat. She was going to let me bury myself there tonight if I gave her my name.

I slid in a second finger. "Reve."

"Reve," she moaned, my name sounding so sweet coming from her parted lips.

I moved her to the other side of the tub, lifting her onto the edge where the wall and window met. She gasped as I spread her apart and dove into her with my tongue. One of her hands gripped my head and the other went to the window, bracing herself as she moved against my mouth.

I slid my tongue up to her clit and swirled my tongue around it, making sure to hit it with my tongue ring. She gasped and her fingers nearly ripped the hair out of my scalp.

"Take me to bed," she breathed.

I whisked us to the bed and settled between her legs, my fingers threading through her hair. Tonight I would do things her way, but I couldn't wait to tie her up and shatter everything she thought she knew about pleasure.

I took her lips with mine and explored her mouth with my tongue, my tongue ring gently hitting her teeth. She gasped at the sensation and I pulled away to stare down at her. Her brown eyes sparkled with desire.

She reached between us and grabbed my cock, guiding it to her entrance and thrusting her hips up to take me inside of her. Fuck, maybe she'd be the one tying me up.

I took over and pulled out so only the head of my cock was inside of her and slammed back into her. Her hands went to the sheets and fisted them as I drove inside of her again and again. Our skin slapped together with heat and sweat.

"Reve, I need more."

I wasn't sure how to give her more without turning this from a fantasy to a nightmare.

I pulled out and flipped her over, taking her from behind. She buried her face in the pillows to muffle her screams. I grabbed her around the waist and pulled her up, her back against my chest. I wanted to hear her scream my name more than anything in the world.

"You wanted to know my name. Let me hear it," I ground out between clenched teeth as I moved her forward and put her hands on the headboard.

"Reve," she moaned, my fingers working against her clit. "Oh God, yes!"

She clenched around me so hard as she came. I exploded inside of her not being able to help myself. If dream sex was this good with her, I couldn't fathom what sex with her awake would be like.

We collapsed into a heap on the mattress, her head resting on my heaving chest. She sighed in satisfaction and traced my screaming skull tattoo with her fingertip.

"You have interesting tattoos. I don't know whether to be scared of them or intrigued by them," she commented, moving a finger over one of my nipple rings. It sent a jolt straight to my dick. We didn't have time for a round two so I willed it to behave.

I kissed her forehead. "We have to leave soon."

"I don't want you to leave." She sat up and looked down at me, her hair falling over her shoulder. I brushed it out of the way, my knuckles light touching her soft skin.

I didn't want to leave either.

I pulled her back onto my chest and smoothed her hair until she fell asleep.

A SMALL, satisfied smile graced her lips as I watched her sleep in Tobias's arms. I would give anything to be able to hold her as he was. But I knew we could never have what they had.

Chapter Seven

Danica

*M*y eyes felt heavy as I opened them at the sound of my alarm clock. I had such a restful Spring break, but last night was torture trying to sleep. Every time my eyes closed I saw death. Except when I dreamed about Reve, but those dreams didn't seem to happen nearly enough.

I pulled myself out of bed and dragged myself to the shower to try to wake myself up. I could really go for a Diet Dr. Pepper but I was almost two months sober.

As the warm water cascaded over my body, I couldn't help but think of Reve. Several nights in a row I had dreamed of Capri, Italy. The first night was mind blowing sex with an orgasm that was so powerful it could really only happen in a dream.

Then we had spent the day on a yacht in the Bay of Naples, laying naked in the sunshine.

A pang of guilt surged through me and I opened my eyes. I shouldn't have been fantasizing about another man, even if imaginary, when I already had three almost perfect ones. Almost being that they currently treated me like a fragile fucking porcelain doll. I guess in a way I was.

I stepped out of the shower and dried off. I might need to give coffee another shot if I wanted to survive my current state of sleep deprivation. Asher's assholishness suddenly made perfect sense to me, although lately he had been more cheerful. More alive than I'd ever seen him. I guess getting your angel wings back had that effect. More likely it was Olly's doing though.

I slid into my uniform and shoved a granola bar in my mouth as I exited my room. I was running late. I made it to class with minutes to spare and slid in next to Olly who was scrolling through his phone.

"Good morning," he mumbled, not looking up from the screen.

I leaned over and tried glancing at what had captivated his attention. He was never glued to his phone and he put it away quickly. I narrowed my eyes at him as he looked up with an innocent expression on his face, but his eyes looked worried.

"What is it?" I couldn't help but let the concern creep into my voice. We had just gotten back some semblance of normalcy if you ignored the fact that I was part of a prophecy and my mother was apparently Lilith.

"After class," he mumbled as Tobias entered the room looking pissed off.

Now I was really concerned. Class passed in a blur of information. Tobias didn't even glance in our direction. Why did I get the feeling that I had done something somehow?

After the class emptied, Tobias leaned against the edge of his desk in front of us and crossed his arms over his chest. I could feel the tension radiating from him, similar to the tension when I had almost gotten us captured at the abandoned hospital.

"What did I do?" For once in my life I literally had no clue what I had done.

Tobias shook his head and then ran a hand over his face before pushing off his desk to stand fully. "You didn't do anything, Danica. Several pictures of us returning to campus last night were taken and posted."

My stomach clenched and I felt nausea swirl in my gut. Olly and I weren't that big of a deal, but Tobias and I? A big fucking deal. Especially since last night he had been carrying me when we returned from Asher's.

"Dean Whittaker has requested a meeting with the three of us this afternoon after classes are over. Until then, please try to keep a low profile. Both of you." Tobias looked between me and Olly, his eyes all business.

"What if I say we got drunk and I called you because I couldn't carry her? Asher made that suggestion," Olly said furrowing his eyebrows.

I turned towards him and gave him a pointed look. "How did Asher know about this before I even did?"

Olly shrugged and pulled his bag over his shoulder. "I texted him."

I shook my head and turned back to Tobias who was regarding Olly with a look of curiosity.

"Let's just see what she says first before we go down that route. You two better get going before you're late for your next class." Tobias moved around to the other side of his desk and plopped down in the chair.

He didn't glance up as we left the room.

On my way out of Uriel Hall, I stopped at the bathroom. Our meeting with the dean was one more thing to add to the shit storm that seemed to be my life. All because I punched John in his nose like he deserved.

After using the restroom, I stepped out of the stall, washed my hands, and then splashed cold water on my face. I heard the door open and glanced in the direction of the sound, water dripping from my face as I grabbed a paper towel from the dispenser. Of course the damn thing got stuck and I had to nearly break off a finger turning the knob on the side.

"Danica Deville, what a pleasant surprise running into you," Betty, the newest Divine, sneered as she came to a stop in front of me. "Cleaning Mr. Armstrong's cum off your face?"

Betty was even bitchier than the rest of the female Divine 7. The men had at least called a cease fire in their attempts at squashing my spirit. They must have been hard pressed for guardian angels to let them stick around. Or their inner bitch hadn't overshadowed whatever light they possessed.

If they expected perfection, there would literally be no angels.

I rolled my eyes at her and moved towards the door, but she stepped in my way. I frowned and she pulled out her phone and flashed a picture of Olly kissing me goodnight while I was still in Tobias's arms.

I remembered the moment. Tobias's eyes had flared with heat as he watched us kiss. I was glad you couldn't see that in that particular picture.

"I don't know what sick game you're playing, Eve, but angels are off limits to your kind." She put her phone away before I could think of snatching it from her, which was probably a good thing.

"Sounds like you're jealous. By the way, jealousy isn't a good look on you, *Beatriz*." I pushed past her and heard her make a noise in her throat as I left the bathroom. Someone needed to knock the Divine down a peg or two.

In most of my classes I was met with stares, but nothing unusual. I was already regarded as some kind of exotic animal on display, now the pictures just added a new layer of intrigue for the masses.

With the warmer weather, Cora, Ethan, Olly, and I ate outside under a tree to avoid any run-ins with the Divine 7.

"How was Cabo?" I asked Cora. Ethan and Olly were engaged in a heated debate about who the Gargoyle King was on *Riverdale*.

"It was great. We pretty much got to party. We had to stay sober, but it was still a blast. I wish you could have come." She picked a blade of grass and rubbed it between her fingers. "I wish Brooklyn would have been able to too."

I know it was a ludicrous thought, but I somehow felt responsible for what had happened to Brooklyn. If only I had stopped her from going out with Levi. She would have hated me, but at least she wouldn't have been tortured at the hands of the Fallen.

And my mother.

When I walked into the library at the end of the day, Olly was already situated in our corner. I smiled and sat in the leather chair next to him, pulling out my binder. We were almost done reviewing the ins and outs of Los Angeles Celestial Academy.

I could have easily read the binder in a day and taken the test that was specially created just for me, but studying with Olly was quite enjoyable.

"Ready for a fun filled hour?" I kicked his leg because he was on his phone again. "Are you addicted to that now or something?"

He put his phone away with a smile on his face and looked at me. "Was just texting Asher."

"Oh really? What's going on with you two? Did I miss something?" I asked, pulling out my notebook and Flair pens. I was glad I had remembered to put them in my bag today; usually I left them in my room.

Olly shrugged. "I've been sleeping on the couch with him. He thinks he's ready to try the bed with us."

My eyes widened and then teared up. Asher never slept in the bed when any of us were over out of fear of having a nightmare and hurting one of us in his sleep. If Olly could help him with his magical soothing touch, I was all for it. "That's really sweet of you. So, you two cuddle?"

Olly let out a laugh and opened his binder to the section we were on. "I guess you could call it that. Why? Does that bother you?"

"No. It's kind of hot thinking of you together like that." I leaned over and looked at what page he opened to and opened my binder. "And if you two wanted to take things further or whatever, I wouldn't be opposed."

"I'm not sure Asher likes me like that." Olly cleared his throat and looked at his binder. "We're onto the good stuff in the binder now. Before the end of this school year, you'll take an aptitude test to see which guardian path best suits you. Healer, warrior, intellectual, or spiritual. Asher and Tobias were both warrior guardians, but when Asher fell, Tobias requested a transfer to intellectual."

"What kind do you think you are?" I was trying to stop the worry from eating me alive. I was really more curious at what the test would say about me since I wasn't an angel. I felt like I was just biding my time at the academy until they figured out what to do with me.

"I don't take the test since I'm an archangel; I'm all of them. Although sometimes I don't feel like it." A flash of sadness passed over his eyes. "Everyone is disappointed in me because I lost that stupid cup."

I suppressed a smile that threatened to come out at the mental image of a wave crashing into him and sending the Holy Grail to the depths of the Pacific Ocean. It was a harsh punishment to be cast out of heaven for such a trivial occurrence. After the conversation with my dad about him being some kind of balance, I wondered if the cup was the only thing that led to his arrival on Earth.

We finished up the section on different types of guardians and packed up our belongings. It was time to face Dean Whittaker, who'd had it out for me from the beginning.

We arrived at the administration offices before Tobias and waited in chairs outside the dean's office. Olly seemed calm and collected, while I was a nervous wreck. If I hadn't just painted my nails, I'd have been chewing on them again.

Tobias walked in right as the minute hand clicked straight up and sat down on the other side of Olly. None of us spoke and Tobias was bouncing his knee. He was just as nervous as I was. It occurred to me he might lose his job over this. Then what would he do? Work on Asher's construction crew gutting kitchens?

"Dean Whittaker will see you now," the secretary said from her desk, gesturing to the closed door.

We stood in unison and I opened the door, walking inside first. Sue Whittaker sat at her desk, pen tapping on the surface, frown on her face. She was not a very inviting person to say the least.

The three of us sat down in chairs in front of her desk and waited for her to strike. If I had learned anything over the past several months, it was to bite my tongue, especially with people like her.

"I'm sure you are all aware of the pictures that surfaced overnight of your clandestine rendezvous outside the staff living quarters. Care to explain?"

"I-" Tobias started to speak but Olly cut him off.

"It's my fault, ma'am. I asked Danica to go to a party with me and we got drunk. I couldn't fly back with her and I called Mr. Armstrong to come get us."

"Are you and Ms. Deville seeing each other now?" She set her pen on her desk and crossed her arms over her ample chest.

"I really don't think that's of your concern, Sue." Tobias crossed his arms over his chest to match her posture and looked between Olly and me. "What they do with their personal time is their own business."

She laughed, but not because it was funny. It was a pissed off laugh. "There is no 'personal time' as you put it, when it comes to being a guardian. Need I remind you that Ms. Deville is not even technically an angel and that relationships with humans are strictly forbidden. Not to mention that she herself is a product of a human and angel indiscretion."

"If you'd like to discuss this further, I suggest you speak with Michael." Tobias stood and looked at us. "We're done here. Let's go."

I was grateful he was taking the lead because I was bound to say something stupid and get myself into trouble. I stood and followed Olly out the door with Tobias trailing behind. He slammed the door behind him and I flinched.

We walked in silence out of Ariel Hall and Olly split away from us, heading back to his room to study.

"Why don't you go change and then come to my

room. I'll help you study and cook dinner so you don't have to eat in the dining hall." Tobias finally spoke when we were mere feet from the staff's building.

The longer I lived in the staff building, the more I hated it. At first I liked living down the hall from Tobias, but now I felt I was always sneaking around in order to not be seen by the other staff members. When I did run into them, they weren't exactly friendly, instead pretending I was invisible. Well, all except Tobias.

"I'm really tired. I think I might just call it a day." I walked ahead of him to the door and he grabbed my wrist, stopping me. I turned back towards him and looked around, hoping no one was looking. "What?"

"It's barely four o'clock. You're coming over." His head tilted slightly to the side and the smallest of smiles turned up the corners of his mouth.

"You aren't the boss of me, Mr. Armstrong." I had the impulse to stick my tongue out at him and run, but held it in. I was eighteen years old, not eight.

He yanked my arm and pulled me to his chest. He bent his head so his mouth was right next to my ear. My heart was hammering from such a public display of affection, especially after the picture fiasco.

"What did you call me?" His lips barely brushed my ear and a zing went straight to my clit.

"Mr. Armstrong. Ow!" He bit my earlobe before pulling it into his mouth. "You're naughty. I need to find my ruler to keep you off me."

He pulled away, his eyes simmering with an unspoken promise of what was to come.

"Is that a threat?" he asked, taking his keys out and opening the door. "Because I'm the only one who will be doing any spanking."

We walked quietly through the common room together, my face heating up as a few sets of eyes landed on us. Tobias was a well-liked teacher among students and other staff. I doubted any of them would say anything even if they did see something. Or maybe they would since it was me.

I changed quickly, throwing on a pair of pajama bottoms and a tank top. Only the best for Tobias. I grabbed my bag and headed down the hall to his room, letting myself in.

Tobias was already in a pair of gray sweats with no shirt and was watching the Dodgers. I dropped my bag on his coffee table and sat next to him.

"Why do you like the Dodgers so much?" I looked over at him and resisted the urge to run my fingers along his muscular stomach. His abs were just barely peeking through his skin. And those sweatpants. Good god, a man in gray sweats was sexy as hell.

He put his hand between my thighs, resting it there. "My dad took me to games at Ebbets Field.

Used to cost about a dollar. I was never able to take my sons to a game."

"Tell me about them," I said softly. "You never talk about your past."

He grunted and looked over at me before turning back to the game. He was quiet for several minutes before deciding to speak.

"I don't talk about my past because it hurts. Unlike Asher who willingly enlisted, I didn't. I ended up being one of the unlucky twenty-percent of those in the draft and left a wife and three small children behind." He looked down at his right arm. He pointed to the woman. "Margaret, everyone called her Margie. I called her Sugar Hips. It drove her crazy, especially when we were out in public. We were high school sweethearts, got married the summer after we graduated."

I ran my finger along her portrait. "She's beautiful. You were a lucky man."

He smiled and pointed to the twins. "Jeffrey and Charlie. They were both precocious and kept us on our toes. I think I got a few gray hairs because of them. Jeffrey became a lawyer and Charlie a history teacher."

"Like you."

"Like me." He cleared his throat and moved his hand down to stroke the portrait of the baby girl. "Sarah. She was the sweetest baby. I wish I would have had more time with her."

I put my head on his shoulder. I wanted to know

more but could hear a slight tremor in Tobias's normally steady voice. I was surprised he told me as much as he had.

"Are you going to study?" He leaned forward and grabbed my bag off the table, changing the subject and breaking the tension. "You're doing decent in your classes. A very reliable source says you have an A in Demonology."

"The only A I've ever gotten was in PE. I hope I earned it." I didn't mean for it to come out like it did. I hoped he graded me just like he did everyone else.

"You've earned your A. You know more than I do. I'm starting to feel a little concerned about my job. You should be the one teaching Demonology."

If he only knew just how close I was to the demon world, he'd probably have re-thought his comment about me teaching at an angel school.

Chapter Eight

*B*y Wednesday, I was beyond exhausted. I texted Asher before he got off work and told him I was staying with him that night. Since I had a key, I drove the thirty minutes to his place with music blaring. I shouldn't have been driving, but I was desperate.

Pulling into the small lot next to the building, there was a motorcycle parked in the spot I usually pulled into. It was one of those crotch rockets that thought they owned the road. I made a face at the bike. They scared the crap out of me when they came zooming between stopped traffic.

It wasn't that I owned that spot, but when you get used to always parking in the same space, you do kind of feel like someone stole it. I pulled into the next available spot, although I was very tempted to park where Asher parked his truck. I'd never hear the end of it though.

I slung my duffel bag over my shoulder and made my way to the stairs. I stopped short at the 'For Rent' sign in the window of the front unit. I backed up and peeked into the slightly open blinds of the window.

From what I could see, it held the same industrial look as Asher's place, but was more of an apartment style with separate living and sleeping spaces. It was the perfect space for a young woman.

An ill-formed plan took hold in my head. I didn't really need to think about it. I took out my phone and dialed the administrative offices at the academy.

"Judy speaking, how may I help you?" I cringed at the secretary's nasally voice.

"Hi Judy. This is Danica Deville. I have a question for you. Am I allowed to live off campus?" I bit my lip and pleaded with heaven above that it was possible. This was too perfect being right downstairs from Asher. I practically lived here anyway.

"Let me speak with Dean Whittaker. Just a moment." She put me on hold. The music playing sounded like it was composed in heaven and I rolled my eyes.

It wouldn't be so bad driving to campus every day and I would finally feel a bit of relief from always being under a microscope. Tobias and Olly wouldn't be happy, but they had wings and could get here in no time.

"Danica?" The secretary came back on the line.

"She said she will approve it. She thinks it is a great idea." Of course Sue Whittaker would think it was a great idea, she hated my guts. She'd have hated me even more if she knew I had demon blood in me. They probably wouldn't even let me attend the academy.

I hung up and then dialed the number for the rental agency that was listed on the window sign. The woman that answered was enthusiastic and said she had just rented out the other unit the day before. That explained the motorcycle.

She arranged to meet me in an hour for a tour and I let out a squeal after hanging up with her. It would be amazing to have a place of my own where I didn't have to worry about eyes being on me.

As I turned and headed for the stairs, I saw the curtains next door fall back into place and stopped short. I guess I had been a little loud.

An hour later I was touring the downstairs unit with the rental broker. It was one bedroom with a large open concept living space. It was a beautiful space, which I knew it would be since Asher had remodeled it.

I filled out paperwork, gave her a deposit, and headed back upstairs. Asher's truck was parked in his spot. He was probably wondering where I was.

I opened the door and smelled the familiar scent of his shampoo—pineapple and coconut—wafting through the air. He was standing at his dresser, his towel in a heap on the floor at his feet. Asher after a shower was always too much for my libido. It was an instant turn on, the small droplets of water were still sitting on his skin. I wanted to lick them off.

"There you are. Where were you? You missed out on a shower." He pulled a pair of basketball shorts out of a drawer and slid them on.

I licked my lips and kept my eyes on his chest as he pulled a shirt over his head. With a body like that, he shouldn't be allowed to wear a shirt, ever.

"When you look at me like that, it's like you've never seen me naked before." He picked up his towel and made his way towards me. "Are you going to answer me or just stand there and stare?"

"What's wrong with staring? I'm making up for lost time." I sometimes found myself staring at him, still not believing he was actually back and alive.

He pulled me in for a quick kiss before hanging up his towel in the bathroom. I followed him into the kitchen where he got out a beer.

"I was downstairs getting a tour and filling out papers for the front rental," I finally said, answering the question he had asked me when I first walked in.

He paused with the bottle halfway to his lips and stared at me for a moment before taking a drink. "And why is that?"

I rolled my eyes and took the beer out of his hand, putting it on the counter. I stepped into him and put my hands on his chest.

"I can't stay on campus anymore. Please support

me in this because Tobias is going to flip the fuck out."

"As he should. Did you even think this through all the way?" His expression was neutral as he examined my face, his eyes lingering on the dark circles under my eyes. "We are all worried about you. I don't think it's a good idea for you to be on your own."

I stepped away from him and gathered my hair in a pony tail, wrapping the elastic that had been on my wrist around the handful of hair. In a way he was right, but what if being alone was exactly what I needed?

"I'm eighteen years old, and I've had plenty of experience being on my own. Summer break is only a few weeks away anyways and I don't plan on staying on campus or in Montecito all summer by myself. This is the best move for me." I folded my arms across my chest.

"You can stay here. With me." He put his hands on my hips and looked at me seriously.

I raised my eyebrows. "You can't just sleep on the couch all the time. Besides, you have no walls. I need walls."

"Walls are overrated. So you're saying you wouldn't want to live here with me?" He stuck out his bottom lip in a mock pout. "You wound me."

I was shocked he would even suggest me moving in with him. That would completely change the group dynamic if I decided to live with one over the others. Plus, even though I loved him, I still needed privacy.

"What about Olly?" I propped my hip against the counter and watched as his face twisted in surprise at my question.

"What about him?" Asher grabbed his beer and took a long drink.

"Don't you want him to move in too?" He tensed up slightly and walked over to get another beer, even though he wasn't completely done with the first.

"Do you want something to drink?" he asked, avoiding my question. I shook my head and watched him open another beer. He had been drinking less lately, but still drank more than he probably should.

"I fully support anything you and Olly feel towards each other. Or do with each other."

He leaned against the counter and examined the label on his beer bottle. "It just kind of snuck up on me. I don't want to be unfaithful to you. Not that I'd have sex with him or anything."

I furrowed my brows. "You wouldn't be unfaithful. You don't feel I'm cheating when I'm with Olly or Tobias, do you?" He shook his head, a chunk of his hair falling in his face. I brushed it behind his ear. "I'd be okay with any of you hooking up with each other. No one else though. Makes me feel like a hypocrite since I'm with three men."

"Really what it makes you is one hell of a lucky

woman." He held his beer bottle by the stem and traced his index finger around the rim, his eyes focusing on his movement. "What has Oliver said to you?"

"Maybe you need to talk to him. Figure things out. Life's too short to have regrets," I suggested, placing my hand on his arm.

"It might make things complicated between us. We have a good thing going right now. Why add *that* into the mix?"

"Because it's what you both want. If you're worried about whether you're top or bottom, I'm sure you're a top." I couldn't help the smile that spread across my face at the mental image. "Just make sure you stretch him out beforehand."

I pushed it too far and watched as he visibly shut down, his hand gripping his beer. "Jesus Christ, Dani," he bit out, moving towards the stairs leading to the roof. "This is a big deal and you're joking about anal."

I watched his retreating back as he made his way up the metal stairs and stopped at the door, his hand on the handle. I can't say I was surprised our conversation had led to him escaping. It was what he did when his feelings got too intense or uncomfortable. It was as if he had reached his quota on intense emotions and couldn't stomach anymore.

It had to be a lot to process, the idea of being with a man when for so long he had only been with women.

"Are you coming?" He looked down at me.

"I didn't think I was invited. You're acting all butt hurt. No pun intended." I bit my lip and stifled a laugh. I was evil, I was sure.

He rolled his eyes and left the door open for me to follow.

~

FALLING asleep was easy when you knew your dreams would be sweet instead of torturous. Despite how much I loved my *good* dreams, I was getting more and more suspicious of their source. It didn't stop me from wanting to spend all my time in the only place I could have them.

I stood on the rooftop, the wind blowing my hair into my face. Dark gray storm clouds rolled overhead. The faint rumble of thunder in the distance matched the intensity of my thudding heart.

Tobias, Asher, and Oliver stood before me, their backs ramrod straight, their faces devoid of emotion. Except their eyes. Their eyes stared back at me with hate and disgust.

"Please, don't do this. It shouldn't matter!" I pleaded with them, taking a step forward. They met my advance with a step back. "I love you!"

"We don't love you. Not anymore." Tobias's lip curled off his teeth in a sneer. He was disgusted by me.

This couldn't be happening. They said they loved me and now they were going to leave me. I needed to wake up, I needed to get out of this before my heart shattered.

Their wings snapped open as I sank to my knees on the wet surface of the roof. The rain had started to fall, soaking my clothes, covering the tears streaming down my face. I shivered, but I wasn't sure if it was from the chill seeping into my body from the rain or from my heart breaking.

"I could never love a demon. You disgust me." Asher clenched his fists at his side. "Let's go before she ruins us."

A sob shook my body and my hands braced against the rough surface of the roof. My heart felt as if it was being ripped from my chest.

"Wait." Oliver stepped towards me and kneeled next to me. I knew I could rely on him to see the good in this situation. He was my bright light in the darkness.

I sat back on my heels and he leaned forward, close to my ear. "You're nothing to me."

His words cut like a knife and he backed away before the three angels shot into the sky. The sky lit up with lightening and the thunder shook the roof.

I screamed into the sky, my throat burning with the force. Flames erupted around me as I stood and tilted my head towards the darkened sky.

"Danica." The soft voice came from behind me.

I spun around, the flames intensifying around us. It felt like I had set the whole world on fire. "Where have you been?" I choked out through my tears.

"I'm sorry I'm late, I was..." He didn't complete his thought and he reached forward. I backed away.

"No. You don't get to touch me. Not anymore."

"Danica." His voice held a warning as I backed away another step, closer to the flames.

"Why are you here, Reve?" The flames began swirling up into the sky, like mini tornados.

"I'm here because I love you."

I tilted my head back and laughed and then choked on the sound. I clutched my chest as the gaping hole opened wider.

"You aren't even real. I don't want you here anymore. I don't need you! Leave!" I yelled as the sound of the flames made my voice difficult to hear.

"Danica." My body shook as my name left his lips, sadness in his eyes.

"Danica." A hand was shaking my shoulder. "Baby, wake up."

I sat up abruptly, my head smashing into Asher's. The sharp pain in my forehead ripped me back to reality. I gasped in air, trying to clear my lungs of the empty sensation that had taken hold.

My eyes burned with tears and sweat, blurring my vision and leaving me wondering if I was still in the nightmare. Asher didn't touch me, but sat close to me, ready to comfort me. My vision was starting to clear and I caught a flash of a retreating back in my peripheral vision.

Dark green eyes stared at me from across the railing surrounding the bedroom. He kept his eyes locked on mine as he slowly backed away. My eyes went wide as his legs disappeared, then his torso, and right before Asher swung his head in that direction, his face.

"Reve." The name left my lips as I crawled off the bed and stumbled in the direction he had disappeared. I stood in the spot and wrapped my arms around myself as if that would help me hold myself together.

"Reve? Like an engine?" Asher came to stand in front of me, concern wrinkling his features. "Did you have a nightmare about the Fallen taking you?"

I took a step back from him and shook my head. Had I been screaming in my sleep? My throat felt scratchy and dry. I brushed past him and walked into the kitchen. I grabbed a bottle of water out of the refrigerator and gulped it down, staring at the *SpongeBob SquarePants* picture hanging by a magnet.

"Do you want to talk about it?" Asher asked, standing near the table.

I threw the empty water bottle into the sink and turned to face him, leaning against the counter. My heart rate was returning to normal and the air chilled my sweaty skin. I shivered and Asher stepped forward. I let him.

"I thought your nightmares were under control when you were here." I let Asher wrap his arms around me and lead me over to the couch. He pulled his blanket around me and sat next to me, tucking me under his arm.

I shook my head and let out a shaky breath. *Reve.* Reve was the one keeping the nightmares away. It made so much sense now that I thought about it. He couldn't get onto campus without permission (which he would *never* get) and he didn't know about Montecito. The thought had first snuck into the corner of my mind when Asher was in Montecito but I still had nightmares.

"I dreamed that I was a demon and you all left me." I put my head against his chest as his hand rubbed my arm through the blanket. "And then the whole world was burning around me."

"Hey," he said softly, tilting my chin up to meet his eyes. "Nothing would make me leave you. Nothing."

I nodded, not believing his words but not wanting to explain to him my insecurities. People said those things all the time, yet there was always *something* that would cause a person to leave.

I leaned into him and shut my eyes.

"I think there's been a dream demon in my dreams," I mumbled, barely audible even to myself. I felt his hand tighten on my arm before continuing to rub slowly back and forth. "He has been taking me out of the nightmares, but he was too late this time. I got mad at him."

"A dream demon?" Asher sounded confused. "What do you mean he takes you out of them? Aren't they supposed to cause nightmares or make them worse?"

My hand found his free one and intertwined our fingers before I continued. "He pulls me from my nightmares and takes me to all kinds of places like fancy parties, Disneyland, the beach, Italy. I thought I had just made it all up in my head as an escape. It made no sense until I saw him when I woke up just now." I didn't mention the part about him taking me to bed in some of the most lavish hotels I had ever seen in the past few dreams.

Asher stiffened behind me. "You need to tell your father."

My heart sped up. "You can't say a word about this, Asher. He doesn't hurt me. My dad will kill him if he finds out. I need him."

"He's a demon." Asher sighed and leaned back on the couch, examining my face. "What if he comes back and hurts you?"

That was a good question and one I didn't have an answer to. I didn't know why Reve was around. All I knew was that I needed him.

Chapter Nine

*T*was sure Asher thought I was losing my mind when I decided to just up and practically move in with him until my lease started in the space downstairs. One week of cohabitating with a man that hadn't lived with anyone in decades was something akin to intruding on a bear's den.

Sure, we usually stayed with Asher on the weekends, but an entire week, seven days, was asking the man who preferred to be alone, a lot.

Typically on the weekends Asher had his place cleaned up. It quickly became apparent to me that Asher was a slob.

A sexy slob, but the pile of dirty clothes he left in the bathroom on a daily basis was a constant reminder that being around me, Tobias, and Olly was a chore for him.

He was fine at first, but as the days passed, it became clear to me that Asher needed his space. It probably didn't help that I wanted to binge watch *Gilmore Girls* and he wanted to binge *The Office*. Naked. With a drink in his hand.

His naked binge watching made it rather difficult to study for my finals which were the following week. I would be taking notes and hear him laugh, which always caused me to look up. Even though I knew he was sitting there naked, it still surprised me every damn time my eyes glimpsed the sight and I would spend several minutes gawking.

After a week of sharing his space and existing on takeout I decided to cook. My history with cooking was sketchy. Ramen and frozen foods were about all I could manage. I never had a reason to cook growing up, my caregivers always cooked for me.

They should really make Home Economics a mandatory class in high school. Learning how to cut an onion is much more useful than learning the parts of a cell or the Pythagorean theorem. If there was a zombie apocalypse neither of those things would help me survive. Cooking would though. Well, unless there was nothing left to cook.

After classes ended for the day, I hustled to the grocery store on the way home, since home did not include an all you can eat smorgasbord of food. I could still eat in the dining hall if I wanted, but I didn't particularly want to hang around campus until they served dinner.

I walked through the sliding doors of the

grocery store and grabbed a cart. I came prepared with a list after watching YouTube videos the night before when I couldn't sleep. I was also going to cheat a bit by not actually making anything from scratch.

My goal wasn't to kill my boyfriends.

I stopped in front of the packaged salad and scanned the thirty different mixes. Clearly other people were just as lazy as I was and couldn't even cut their own lettuce. Why else would they have so many? I grabbed a Caesar salad kit, considered who I was feeding, then grabbed a second.

I was feeling pretty good with my two bags of salad until I turned down the pasta aisle. It had to be at least twenty feet of shelving filled top to bottom. And that was just the actual pasta, not the sauce choices.

I'd been in a grocery store before, but it had been a while since I'd been shopping anywhere besides the frozen food section and cereal aisle. I couldn't be the only eighteen-year old to feel lost in a grocery store.

"What the hell am I supposed to do? Eeny meeny miny moe?" I mumbled to myself as I grabbed a bag of rigatoni and examined the back.

"If I may make a suggestion," a woman said from behind me.

I turned and raised my eyebrows at her intrusion on my pasta selection activities.

"Do I know you?" She was dressed in a red

power suit, heels that screamed "fuck me," and had long dark hair that left me feeling hair envy.

"I don't think so. Are you cooking for someone special?" I nodded. She glanced at the pasta box I was holding before plucking it from my hands and putting it back on the shelf. "In the refrigerated section they have pasta and sauces that are far superior to anything you can find down this aisle. I'll help you."

She grabbed my cart and started pushing it in the opposite direction. Who did this woman think she was? I frowned but followed behind her, feeling drawn to her chipper demeanor. Maybe she was just in a good mood and paying it forward.

We stopped in front of the section with prepared pasta and she grabbed the family sized three cheese tortellini and a container of alfredo sauce.

"This is the way to a man's heart, or at the very least, a simple way into his pants." Her red stained lips pulled up into a smile showing her shockingly white, perfect teeth. This woman was walking, talking sex.

"Thanks," I said, watching her as she put them in my cart. "What else should I get? I made a list but I could use all the help I can get."

"Definitely garlic bread, a nice Chardonnay, and something sweet for dessert." She took off again and I followed her.

"I can't buy alcohol," I informed her as we

turned down the wine aisle. She grabbed two bottles and put them in her empty hand basket she had been toting around. She winked at me, her blue eyes sparkling.

After gathering the rest of the meal I followed her to the checkout line and purchased my pretty epic date night meal. I hoped I wouldn't burn it. Boiling water couldn't be that hard, could it?

Once in the parking lot the woman handed me the two bottles of wine and refused the cash I tried to give her.

"Consider it a gift."

"Thanks, I really appreciate your help."

She smiled brightly and walked away, her heels clicking on the pavement.

I loaded my car and made it to Asher's with thirty minutes to spare before my dinner dates arrived.

I placed everything on the counter and snapped a quick photo. I sent it to my dad with a text. *Look, I'm going to actually cook something for other people. Supposedly this meal is the way to a man's heart and into his pants.*

I snickered after hitting send, imagining my dad's face as he read it. He almost immediately texted me back. *What made you decide on that particular meal?*

A woman at the store. She was nice, even bought the wine for me.

The typing bubbles appeared and disappeared several times. I put the phone down and preheated the oven for the bread. Preheating an oven was my jam.

The front door opened and slammed shut as I turned on the stove to boil water. I heard Asher drop his keys in the metal bowl by the door and make a grunt as he took off his boots. I didn't need to turn to see him do it, it was the same every day.

"Are you *cooking*?" He seemed to have stopped in his tracks across the room.

I turned after placing the lid on the pot of water just in time to see Asher pull off his shirt and toss it near the wall by the bathroom. He walked towards me and I put my hands up.

"I want it to be a surprise. Go shower. Olly and Tobias will be here in a bit." My eyes moved from his abs up to his face where his eyebrows were raised.

"I need a drink." He started forward again and I met him halfway, stopping him. "At least give me a beer or my bottle of whiskey."

"It will ruin your palate for my meal. We're having wine." I put a hand on his chest and he covered it with his before yanking me the rest of the way towards him and kissing me.

He hadn't even eaten the meal yet and I was halfway into his pants. Not that I needed a reason to ever sleep with any of them. One or more was always willing. But tonight wasn't about that. Tonight was about repaying them for always putting up with my crap.

"You do remember that time you decided to make toast, don't you? There were flames." He traced my bottom lip with his finger and his eyes twinkled. My face started to burn as I recalled my failed attempt at toasting bread.

There weren't flames. There definitely was a lot of smoke that set off the smoke detectors though.

He let me go and opened the cabinet under the sink, grabbing a fire extinguisher from inside.

I frowned as he set the red canister on the counter. "Don't burn down my kitchen."

Smart ass.

He turned and headed towards the bathroom. I grabbed a potholder and chucked it at him. It sailed past him and he turned and smirked. "You missed. I hope your cooking is better than your aim."

I rolled my eyes and turned back to watch the water pot. He was distracting to say the least.

By some miracle I didn't burn anything and the food tasted great. Maybe I could get on board the cooking train if it was really that easy.

"THAT WAS amazing and you know how picky I am," Olly said, putting his fork down on his empty plate and sitting back. He took a sip of his Chardonnay and frowned into the glass. "I don't think I like *this* though."

"It was perfect. What's the special occasion?" Tobias asked, swirling his wine before taking a sip.

I shrugged. "No reason. Just felt like cooking you guys dinner. I was also sick of eating takeout and frozen pizza."

Tobias ran his finger around the rim of his wine glass. "I don't think you should move off campus."

I sighed. This conversation was a daily occurrence in some shape or form. Olly was also not a fan of me moving off campus, but neither man really had a clue what living there was like for me.

"She'll be perfectly fine downstairs. We can even get walkie talkies if it would make you two get off her back." Asher stood and started piling plates to take to the sink. "You can't expect her to stay somewhere that makes her stay in the same building with her teachers."

"They might be willing to let you move to a student building. Let me talk to Sue." I frowned at Tobias and stood to help Asher. Living in a student building would be even worse than living with the teachers.

"Sit. We'll do the dishes," Olly said, standing to help Asher.

"I knew I could count on you, angel baby." Asher grabbed the plates from Olly's hands and took them to the sink. "Unlike Toby. See him sitting over there pretending like we aren't doing the dishes? That's why he approved of this whole harem business, now he has three maids."

I laughed as Tobias ignored Asher's dig. It was true though. Tobias tended to sit back after eating, even when everyone else jumped up to clean.

"I've already signed papers and ordered furniture. I'm not even sure I'm going to continue next year now that I have my GED. The fact that I'm going to have to make up the first semester over the summer is not appealing at all."

"We told you we'd help you with that. You can't just quit, Danica." Tobias frowned and finished his drink.

"Why not? No one there likes me, plus being an angel just isn't in my cards." I turned my attention to Olly and Asher cleaning up the kitchen. Every time Asher handed Olly a plate to put in the dishwasher, their fingers would brush. I wasn't sure who they thought they were fooling, but something special was brewing between them. Maybe they just needed a little push.

"I like you. Oliver likes you. Ethan and Cora like you. Screw the rest of them." He stood and moved behind me, putting his hands on my shoulders and starting to massage them. "I'll miss you."

"Now you guys will know how I felt all these months with her so far away. Imagine how I felt not even able to go to her on campus. You two can at least fly and be here in a few minutes." Asher dried his hands and he and Olly sat on the sectional next to each other.

Tobias moved my hair off my shoulders and

leaned down to kiss my neck. He trailed his lips to my ear and moved his mouth so it was only touching when he spoke. "No more early morning visits."

"You can still visit me in the mornings," I breathed as he flicked his tongue against my ear.

"Not the same." He kissed my temple and pulled me after him to the couch.

I turned back towards the kitchen when my phone buzzed on the countertop. I picked it up, finally seeing a reply from my dad. *Your mother cooked me that same exact meal the night she told me she was pregnant.*

My phone slipped from my hand.

I HAD CONVINCED myself that the woman from the grocery store couldn't have been Lilith. That would mean she was following me. I didn't say a word about it to the guys; they didn't need any reason to try to stop me from moving off campus.

I made my way across the lush campus of Los Angeles Celestial Academy towards the staff building. The grounds were mostly deserted since it was class time and all first years were taking their guardian placement assessment.

I had been the first one done. Whether that was a good sign or a bad sign would be known soon.

Would I be a healer, warrior, intellectual, or a spiritual guardian angel?

The test was a joke, at least for me. I was no angel. I couldn't heal. I wasn't a fighter. I definitely didn't have the brains to be an intellectual. And well, my spiritual beliefs were shaky at best. The test was supposed to determine which courses angels took from second year forward.

I smiled to myself, thinking of the test. It had some ridiculous questions on it. It was mostly multiple choice that tried to gauge interest and personality. My favorite questions were the open-ended ones. In particular the question: *Two people are in a room and you are told one of them has to die. What five questions would you ask to decide who lives and who dies?*

I was certain my response was not what they were looking for at all. I wrote:

What is this, the movie Saw*? First off, I would never be in a room where one of two people has to die. In what world would this happen? I will humor you though. This is assuming the two people don't know that one of them is going to die.*

1. *How would you describe the one person in your life you would die for?*
2. *If you had one day left to live, what would you do?*
3. *Diet Dr. Pepper or Diet Pepsi?*
4. *Dogs or cats?*
5. *Dark chocolate or white chocolate?*

Clearly anyone that answers Diet Pepsi, cats, or white chocolate is a prime candidate for death. Asking who deserves to live or die in any situation is a ridiculous question. I expect better from angels.

MOST OF MY answers were filled with snark. I was sure Olly came up with something that transcended the fine line between morality and immorality.

I changed into jeans and an old shirt once back in my room. I texted Asher that I was done with my test. He had taken half the day off to help me and Olly pack my life and move it to my new place.

Thirty minutes later, I went downstairs to let Asher into the building and to help him carry boxes in. The building was mostly empty since all of the teachers were teaching or scoring the placement assessments.

"You got finished with your test pretty quickly," Asher commented, following me up the stairs. He had to stop halfway to adjust the grip on the stack of boxes he held. "Did it go okay?"

"Everyone stared at me like I was crazy for being done so fast, so probably not. I thought it was better to just answer with my immediate thoughts. I bet I'm in Slytherin." I walked into my room and dropped the broken-down boxes on my bed.

"Slytherin?" I turned and saw the confused look on his face. Was he kidding? He had to be kidding.

He must not have paid any attention at Universal Studios.

I grabbed a box and taped it up. The déjà vu was strong as I pulled the tape gun across the bottom.

"What do you want me to help with?" He grabbed the tape gun from me and taped another box.

I was just about to answer when Olly burst into the room, panting. The door banged against the counter. Asher dropped the tape gun he was holding and cursed.

"Fuck, man! Don't do shit like that!" Asher shook his head and went into the bathroom, slamming the door behind him.

I frowned and put my hands on my hips.

"I didn't know he'd be here yet." He had to take two breaths to get his words out.

"Why are you panting? Did something happen?" I went back to taping boxes. I wanted to check on Asher, but the lock had clicked, meaning he wanted to be left alone.

"Just wanted to see you." He made his way to the bathroom door and knocked gently. "I'm sorry."

There were grumbles in return and Olly turned back to me with a frown. I just shrugged. I was used to the mood swings from Asher. Sometimes they were for a reason, like when something unpredictable happened, but they were also seemingly for no reason.

"Here, why don't you put the crap in my night-stands in this box." I handed him a box and then started emptying my dresser drawers.

"I'm sure none of your stuff is crap," he said as Asher finally came out of the bathroom.

Olly was bent at the waist, his hand starting to open the nightstand when he looked over his shoulder. Asher's eyes were heated as he stared back at Olly. His eyes slid briefly to his ass before turning back to the box he had dropped.

The sexual tension between the two of them was getting worse every time we were together. I didn't know what was holding them back. I had been pretty clear that I wanted them to explore their feelings for each other, but maybe I hadn't been clear enough.

Olly started putting the contents of my night-stand into the box. It mostly contained cords and old notes from Ava.

"What is this?" He held up my purple clit stimu-lator with an amused look on his face. My face heated as both their eyes landed on me.

He pushed the button and it started buzzing, causing him to drop it on the bed. Asher grabbed it and turned it off.

"What would you even need this for?" Asher asked, his eyes widening and glimmering with mischief. "Are the three of us just not doing it for you anymore? We can remedy that pretty quickly."

"When was the last time you jacked off?" I

grabbed it from him and he grabbed my wrist, tugging me towards him.

"In the shower before coming here. I don't see what that has to do with you having a toy." His eyes went to my lips.

"So you can get off without me, but I can't without you?" I laughed and pulled away from him before he could move in to kiss me.

We had packing to do. Not that there was much, but I was more than ready to leave this place in the dust.

"Do you use it often?"

"Lately, no. Now, say two really hot male angels walked in my room and started making out and touching each other. I wouldn't even hesitate to use it." I couldn't stop the smirk that spread across my face as Asher's eyes widened further and Olly made a sound that was half gasp, half choke.

"Do you often get hot angels coming to your room and making out?" Asher moved back to the dresser he was emptying. He grabbed a handful of clothes and put them in a box, avoiding Olly, who was staring at him.

I sat down against my headboard and turned on the toy, the sound filling the quiet room. "Not as often as I'd like."

"Let's say two hot angels did come to your room. Wouldn't you just use *them* instead of that hunk of plastic?" Asher shut the empty drawer and turned to look straight at me, his lips in a tight-line, his eyes darkened by his dilated pupils.

"Maybe, but sometimes it's fun to watch. Especially when they've been eye-fucking each other." I unbuttoned my pants and looked between the two of them. "I don't know what's been holding them back."

The tension in the room escalated, the lust so palpable I could almost reach out and dip my fingers in it. Olly took a step towards Asher who backed against the dresser. This was one of those moments that it felt like the world stopped spinning for everyone except the two men in front of me.

Olly cupped the back of his neck, pulling him closer. His move surprised me, but then again Olly seemed to have turned over a new leaf.

"I don't know if this is-" He didn't even let Asher get the words out before he kissed him hard.

In my head I had imagined their first kiss being a little softer, very PG. I thought it would be Hallmark Channel gentle with U2's *With or Without You* playing in the background. Instead, what I got was stormy, forceful, and enough to melt my panties right off.

Asher put his hands on Olly's shoulders and pushed him slightly. Olly didn't budge, having a few inches and pounds of muscle on him. Asher was stiff as a board, and when Olly finally pulled away, they were both breathing hard.

"Sorry, I-" Olly started, but Asher grabbed him

and spun him so he was pressed against the dresser. The dresser hit the wall and he stared at Olly, one hand bunched in his shirt, the other braced on the edge of the dresser.

I couldn't take my eyes off the two of them, my toy forgotten for the moment. It was like two pit bulls circling each other, waiting to go in for the kill. Olly's eyes landed on me but Asher let go of his shirt and grabbed his chin, bringing his eyes back to him.

They stared at each other for what felt like an eternity, having a silent conversation with their eyes. I knew Olly was open to being with a man, but Asher was a closed book when it was brought up. My stomach dropped as my brain finally processed the fallout that this might cause between all of us.

I shouldn't have pushed them so hard. They weren't ready and I had forced their hand with my flirting and teasing.

I was just about to get off the bed to make sure Asher didn't turn violent when he leaned forward and kissed Olly. My heart thumped hard in my chest as their lips moved against each other, Olly's hand settling on Asher's waist.

Asher pulled away and cleared his throat. "We should finish packing her stuff."

Words must have escaped Olly because he nodded before both he and Asher looked at me on the bed. There was uncertainty written in their eyes, like maybe they thought I'd have an issue with what they just did.

"That was... wow." I stood on shaky legs and threw my vibrator in the box.

They probably didn't need me masturbating to their first kiss, although the wetness between my legs was hard to ignore.

Chapter Ten

$\mathcal{I}$ didn't think it would be too different living in my own place, but somehow, it was. Living on campus never felt right and being in my dad's house never came with the responsibility of taking care of things on my own.

Now I was on my own.

The space was quite large for being a one-bedroom apartment, with an open concept living room and kitchen. The ceilings were high and the windows were the same old factory style as Asher's. The bedroom was probably my favorite because it was large enough to fit a gigantic bed that could easily fit all of us.

The guys hadn't seen the bed yet, and I'm sure their reactions would be priceless.

I plopped down on my couch and hugged a pillow to my chest. Things were finally starting to look up for me. School was almost out and I was going to pass all of my classes. The only problem was that I didn't see what purpose they would serve.

Did the academy offer a course on dealing with your tainted blood?

Did they offer a class on not turning evil?

I stared at my reflection in the blank television screen. The angels at the academy weren't wrong that I had evil blood. They just thought it was my father's. Boy, were they wrong.

I still had to figure out how to tell Tobias, Asher, and Olly about what I knew about my mother and about my own blood. I didn't know who would have a worse reaction.

I pulled myself from the couch, which was absurdly comfortable and had to have some kind of tranquilizing properties, and walked around the island into the kitchen. I was about to start pulling out ingredients to cook when a knock came at my door.

The guys weren't supposed to come over for another hour. I was cooking for them again. The only way to learn is to actually do it. This time I was doing more than boiling water and dumping sauce on pasta.

I walked to the door and looked out the peep-hole. A delivery driver stood outside, a van with 'Beautiful Blossoms' written on the side was behind him. My stomach fluttered and I opened the door. No one had sent me flowers before.

"Danica? I have a delivery here for you." My

eyes went wide as I took in the vase of roses in his hands and the open back door of his delivery van. "Forty-two roses."

"Forty-two?" I took the vase and he turned to grab two more vases.

"He was very specific."

I didn't see a card and twisted my face in thought. "Is there not a card? Who are they from?"

"He was very specific about that too. There isn't a card and I can't give you his name." The man smiled and then got into the van to leave.

I didn't know rose buying protocol, but with crazy stalkers I would have thought a buyer would have to give more information to the recipient. I set the vases on the counter and stared at the roses. Who would send me such a random number?

Maybe he had meant forty-eight. That made more sense. I started counting them. Forty-one. I counted again.

I picked up my phone and sent a group text. *Thanks for the roses, whoever sent them.*

I pulled out the ingredients to make chicken enchiladas. The website I got the recipe off of said only an idiot would mess up the recipe that pretty much was tortillas, canned chicken, sour cream, canned sauce, and cheese. As long as I remembered to set the timer, I was confident I wouldn't be an idiot.

I emptied the cans of chicken in a bowl and added the sour cream. It would probably be better with fresh chicken but there was no way I was risking giving everyone salmonella poisoning due to my poor cooking skills. Plus raw chicken grossed me out.

I checked my phone and frowned down at the responses to my thank you. None of them had sent me roses. Maybe my dad had sent them, although that certainly didn't make any sense.

I laid a flour tortilla on a cutting board and was about to scoop the chicken mixture inside when there was another knock on the door. I wiped my hands on a towel and looked out the peephole.

My heart stopped.

Reve's head was down, but I'd recognize his slicked back hair anywhere. How had he even known where I lived? I gulped down the lump that had suddenly worked its way into my throat and put my shaking hand on the door handle.

When I had told him to leave, he hadn't been back. I didn't quite know how to feel about him standing on the other side of my door in the flesh. Would he be the same as he was in my dreams?

He knocked again and I took a steadying breath before opening the door a crack. He had a hand behind his back, and the other tucked in his front pocket, his thumb in the belt loop of his distressed jeans.

"Hi." His voice was just as soothing as it had always been.

I ran my eyes down his body before meeting his

moss-colored eyes twinkling back at me. He pulled his hand out from behind his back.

"You sent me the roses?" I still hadn't opened the door fully, trying to decide if it was safe. He was a demon.

My shoulders slumped as my own thoughts hit me like a ton of bricks. *I* was a demon too. His slight smile suddenly dropped and his eyes glistened with concern. He could read me like a book. Of course he could; he had been inside my head.

"Yes, I did. Are you okay? You're pale."

I put my hand against my cheek. I stepped out of the way and opened the door.

"It's just, you're real. You're a demon. You were inside my dreams."

Were all demons so attractive?

He blinked a few times and cleared his throat. "Are you going to let me in or should I go?"

I moved to the side and he stepped into the foyer, handing me the rose in his hand. I didn't know what to make of him. He tortured people in their dreams, turning them into nightmares. Yet, here he was, sending me roses.

We stood awkwardly facing each other, the rose acting as a barrier between us. I probably shouldn't just go opening my door to strangers and then letting them inside. He wasn't a stranger though. He knew me more intimately than my boyfriends even did. He knew my worries and fears. He knew my desires.

Besides, he could probably get inside without me even opening the door.

"Do you want something to drink? Do demons eat and drink?" I bit my lip as I stepped back into the kitchen. I didn't know what to say to him.

He stopped at the edge of the counter and propped his hip against it, his legs crossed at the ankles, and folded his arms crossed over his chest. The fabric of his black cotton t-shirt stretched and his biceps poked out from the sleeves.

His arms were covered in tattoos, just like they were in my dreams. The most noticeable tattoos being the chains around his neck and wrists. I hadn't had the balls to ask him about them yet.

"I don't *have* to eat or drink."

I nodded and went back to putting the chicken and sour cream mixture in a tortilla with cheese as if I hadn't just let a demon into my apartment. I could feel his eyes watching me and braved another glance at him.

"Are you cooking for them?" His voice had a hint of jealousy to it. "Maybe I should go."

I shook my head. I finished the last enchilada and dumped the can of green sauce over them and sprinkled grated cheese on top. I was considering what I wanted to say to him as I preheated the oven.

"Why were you in my dreams? Was I even in control? I felt like I was." It really had felt like my feelings and actions were my own.

He hopped up on my counter like he owned the place and his hands wrapped around the edge. I kept my distance, not trusting myself to be closer to him. I was drawn to him, just like I had been in my dreams.

"Forty-two days ago I was over the roof and was drawn to your pain. I couldn't resist a taste since pain and suffering feed me. But when I was in your own nightmare it made me sick. That was the night I asked you to dance." His eyes darkened slightly as he looked at me. "You've always had free will. Well except when you wanted your three boyfriends there. I blocked that."

His expression turned into a smile and my breath caught in my throat. His smile was enough to bring me to my knees. Even here in the flesh, I wanted him.

"We are a package deal." What was I saying? I couldn't just make a decision without making sure the other three were fine with it. My heart stuttered at the thought of them rejecting Reve.

"Toby will be the hardest to convince of my intentions. He is very protective of you." I gave him a confused look and he continued. "Sometimes you are all still awake when I come to you. I observe your interactions. If anyone is going to try to kill me, it will be him. The other two are too caught up in each other that they probably won't care. Toby though, you're his end game."

"Let me take care of Tobias." I looked down at

my hands. "Stay for dinner. Let's see what happens."

What could possibly go wrong? It would be so simple to introduce him as the dream demon who had been wooing me with romantic gestures in dreams. They would totally be on board with me wanting to explore him in the flesh. Totally.

"There's another small problem. Your father can't know about this. If I would have known he was your father I wouldn't have..." He sighed and ran his hand through his hair. "Now I'm in too deep."

"I can't guarantee that." I really couldn't. Sometimes my dad just showed up unannounced. Besides, if I didn't tell him then someone else would, I was sure.

I grabbed my phone. It was better that they were prepared for Reve and not entering blindly. *A dream demon will be at dinner. You better be on your best behavior.*

Reve slid off the counter and walked around the island into the living room. He picked up a few pictures I had and looked at them.

I watched him as he moved around the room before he sat down on the couch, crossing his ankle onto his knee. His movement was much smoother than a human's or even an angel's.

"Do you fly?" I asked. Of course everyone had super powers except me.

"Something like that. It's more of a float and

only when I'm in phantom form." He patted the couch cushion. "Come sit. You set the timer on the oven. You don't have to watch it."

"You cook?"

"No, but I've been around long enough that I know how things work. Like timers." He grinned at me. He was a little bit of a smart ass, something he hadn't been in my head.

I needed to keep him away from Asher.

"How long have you been alive?" I was starting to realize that this question didn't matter much anymore. Not when those around you lived seemingly forever.

"Do you really want the answer to that? It's much longer than your angels." I stood off to the side of the couch and his eyes moved from my face, down my body, and back up. I did the same to him.

"You look twenty." If I had to hazard a real guess, he was much older than twenty. Tobias and Asher were one hundred. He couldn't be that much older.

"In Inferna, we don't measure time. It's hard to say how long I've been alive, if I'm being honest. Are you going to sit? I don't bite. Unless you want me to." He ran his hand over the cushion next to him and then folded his hands in his lap.

I sat down next to him and turned my body towards him. "Inferna?"

"The part that your father runs is referred to as hell, but that's in Inferna. Could you imagine someone saying, 'go to Inferna' instead of 'go to hell?'" He chuckled and shook his head. "Inferna doesn't flow off the tongue like hell does."

"You never said how old you are."

He rubbed his chin, thinking. He looked up at the ceiling and then did some elaborate counting on his fingers, mouthing things to himself. "Maybe around two thousand."

My eyes widened. "We're talking weeks, right?"

"Years. It's an approximation, give or take a century or two."

My mouth opened in disbelief. I didn't even have time to completely process his age, when there was a knock at the door. He went to stand and I put my hand across his chest, stopping him like when you slam the brakes in a car and put your hand out to stop the passenger from flying forward.

This was about to be a car crash.

"I'll get it. Wouldn't want you to fall and break a hip." I stood as he laughed. What else do you say to a demon that is so old?

I felt like puking as I went to the door. They wouldn't try to *kill* Reve, would they? Could Reve even die? Jesus, he was practically older *than* Jesus. Perhaps he *was* older than him.

I opened the door to three concerned faces. At least this time I wasn't covered in bruises. It's the small victories.

"A dream demon sent you roses and is now in your apartment to join us for dinner?" Tobias wasted no time brushing past me and walking right into my living room. He had connected all the dots quickly, although Asher had most likely told him everything already.

Asher followed close behind him, but Olly stopped in front of me as I shut the door. "Did he hurt you?"

My mouth had opened to respond but then I heard a grunt and turned to see Tobias had pinned Reve to the brick wall. Of course, at that moment, the timer for the oven went off.

"Let him go." I stopped several feet away, not knowing if they were going to come to blows. Reve had his hands up in surrender and had an amused look on his face. "Now."

Tobias let him go and stepped back, a scowl on his face. "I think it's time for you to leave."

"*You* can leave, but Reve isn't." I gave him a pointed look and then went to turn off the oven and take out the enchiladas. It was a risky move taking out a hot pan with shaky hands, but somehow I managed to get the Pyrex dish onto the stovetop without burning myself.

"What if he tries to kill us or something?" Olly whispered, suddenly appearing right beside me. I jumped at his sudden appearance next to me. Somehow he managed to move like a tiger going in for the kill.

I slammed the spatula I had in my hand down and turned towards him. "No one is going to kill anyone. Actually, you know what? I take that statement back. I will kill each and every one of you assholes if you don't sit your asses down at the table and shut up."

Olly's eyes went wide before he turned and marched his ass to the table and sat down. I watched as the rest of them sat down silently.

I was tired and irritable and just wanted to enjoy the dinner I cooked, not listen to them berate Reve about being a demon. It was the last thing I wanted to hear.

I let out a shaky breath and dumped a bag of tortilla chips in a bowl, grabbed the premade salsa and guacamole, and put them in the middle of the table. No one said a word but there was still a lot of distrustful looks going on.

How would they react when they knew about me? I shuddered at the thought as I placed the pan of enchiladas on the table and sat down.

We ate in silence, besides the grunts that acknowledged that what I had cooked was actually decent. Maybe there was a future for me in the culinary arts, although all it would take was one squirrel and I would be distracted enough to burn a house down.

I was munching on a chip when Tobias put his fork down and looked between me and Reve. "Have you two slept together?"

The tortilla chip lodged in my throat and I damn near felt like I was going to die. I gulped down half the glass of water in front of me as the chip went down like a knife.

"I don't know how best to answer that question." Reve pushed his plate slightly forward on the table and folded his hands in front of him. "Technically speaking, no."

Tobias's eyes narrowed on Reve. "Either you have or you haven't."

"Well, I have never physically touched her." Reve looked over at me.

"What does that even mean? You've touched her, just not with your hands? I don't speak demon, so you're going to have to clarify." I was a little shocked at how Tobias was speaking to Reve. He was protective of me, but this was a whole new level.

"Aren't you some hotshot teacher? I'd expect a little more from a man that teaches Demonology. You must be one of those that they can't shake because of tenure." My eyes went wide as Reve blasted Tobias. "It means I haven't *physically* touched her. I'm a dream demon. I'm sure you are smart enough to figure out the rest."

My head swiveled back and forth between the two. Reve looked smug and Tobias's face had turned red.

"So you took advantage of her in her dreams?" Tobias put his hands on the table like he was about to stand up. I didn't want him to stand up.

Asher and Olly just sat in silence. They seemed

amused at the back and forth between the two men. At least they weren't attacking Reve too.

"I can assure you that her subconscious made all the decisions to proceed with any sex that was had. Right Danica?"

"Sex that wouldn't have happened if you weren't in her head to begin with."

"Guys, can you please stop." I let out a sigh. "Even in the dreams, I feel the same way as I do with any of you. Protected, loved."

"You think *he's* the fourth guardian?" Tobias scrunched up his nose in disgust. "It's highly unlikely-"

"It actually makes sense. An archangel, a Fallen, a turned angel, a demon." Olly brought his hand to his chin.

"Do they all walk into a bar?" Asher seemed to be the least interested in the whole conversation of sex with Reve. He had the most time to process the whole situation, which gave me hope that Tobias would come around too.

"What?" Olly looked at Asher, shook his head in confusion and turned back to me. "The prophecy never said anything about your guardians being angels."

"I'm not sure why she needs guardians. She is powerful enough to protect herself." Reve looked confused and then turned thoughtful and looked at me. "Must be the angel part of you. Angels have always been the weaker ones."

My eyes widened and my heart stopped for a fraction of a second. Did he know I was part demon? He winked before turning his attention back to a disgruntled Tobias.

"I just don't foresee this working with a demon. We are all angels, and you are most certainly not." Tobias crossed his arms over his chest as if his word was final.

"You love me, don't you?" I asked softly.

"Of course I do." He seemed shocked that I would even ask.

"And you know I love you?" He nodded in reply. "When we started this, *you* were the one that said being with the others was fine. You said you'd be with me no matter what."

"He's a demon, Danica."

"So what? He's taken care of me. Why do you think I always wanted to sleep at Asher's? He was the reason. I just didn't understand that what was happening in my dreams was an actual person."

"You slept with him." Hurt passed over Tobias's eyes.

Should I feel guilty about having sex in a dream? I wasn't sure. "In a dream. I haven't touched him awake, but I think I will now, because we've discussed and I've decided."

There was a moment of silence and Tobias shut his eyes briefly, as if to gather his thoughts and emotions. "So you want this? To have him be a part of our... thing?"

"I believe it's called a harem." Olly was staring at Reve as if trying to get a read on him. I wouldn't be surprised if that was in his skillset too.

"Whatever it's called, I do want to have him be a part of it. The same way I wanted to be close to all three of you. For whatever reason, he's here, with us. I know it seems sudden, but hasn't everything been a bit sudden?" I couldn't help the way I felt. To an outsider, everything was unconventional, but to me it was my normal.

People meet and fall in love quickly all the time. For me, it was just with four men. Four men I was incredibly sexually attracted to as well.

"Would it help if I let you take a swing at me? Violence seems to help alpha males such as yourself move past any hang-ups." Reve smirked across the table at Tobias.

"I'm not an alpha male!" I would have laughed at Tobias's defensiveness if it hadn't been such a serious conversation.

"Dude. You are. Maybe not a loud one or one that pisses all over the place, but you *do* get a bit mental over her." Asher chuckled and ran a hand through his wavy locks. "Olly told me about you freaking out that you couldn't come back to Earth right away when you were summoned to heaven."

"I agree. You are a quiet, brooding dick at times when it comes to her. It's fucking annoying," Olly mumbled.

My eyes widened. "Asher is rubbing off on you."

"They haven't done that yet, have they? Rubbed each other off?" Reve asked, clearly misconstruing my words as a sexual reference. Or maybe he wasn't and he just wanted to instigate a confrontation.

Now that I had seen him interact with others, I was certain it was the latter.

"You *told* him about us?" Asher sighed and looked at me for an answer.

"No." It had only been a day, why would I tell Reve of all people?

"What do you mean *us*?" Tobias seemed to forget about Reve for the moment. He gestured between Olly and Asher. "As in you two... together?"

"It's complicated," Asher responded. "We're still working on the details of what we are."

Olly frowned at Asher's words, but still kept his eyes locked on the side of Asher's head. I didn't know what details needed to be worked out, but it was pretty clear after their kiss the day before that they were about to combust.

I stood and grabbed Tobias's arm because the conversation was headed down the toilet.

"Let's talk in the bedroom." I turned to Reve. "Maybe you can explain yourself to them."

Tobias followed me into the bedroom and I shut the door. His eyes immediately went to the bed.

"Really? They make a bed *this* big? I guess we

kind of need it now that Asher and Oliver are doing whatever and you seem to be convinced that a demon could be one of your guardians. Have you told your dad about this yet?"

"No, and you aren't going to. I will tell him." He made a noise in his throat. "What's going through your head?"

"Well, let's see. You've been abducted and almost died in a basement used for bleeding out angels. Then you decide to steal medical files and get the shit beat out of you. You irrationally move off campus. And now there's Reve, a demon. What is supposed to be going through my head? I love you, and I want to protect you, but you are making it so fucking hard."

Tears sprung to my eyes. When he said all the facts in a nice succinct way, he had a point. I sat on the edge of the bed.

"Are you breaking up with me?" I wouldn't blame him if he was. Out of all of them, he was the one I worried would leave the most. We were an unlikely pair, and despite it feeling so natural between us, sometimes I wondered if he felt the same.

"No. Why would you even jump to that conclusion?" He sat down next to me and ran his fingers through his hair and then rested his elbows on his legs, his face in his hands. "The thought of something happening to you terrifies me." He shook his head slightly. "I can't lose another family."

I put my hand on his back and let out a shaky sigh. "You aren't going to lose me, or Asher, or Olly. I'm sure eventually you will feel better about Reve."

He turned his head towards me, his hands resting on one side of his face. The eye that I could see was swimming with tears and one dripped out and onto his jeans. I bit my lip to keep my own tears from spilling over.

"You can't know that for sure. We all know something is coming. When it does, what if..."

"That's why I have guardians, right? There's no use in worrying about it when instead we could be spending that time loving each other. I mean, look at this bed," I joked.

He snorted and rubbed his eyes with the palms of his hands before sitting up straight and pulling me towards him into a hug. "I don't trust him." He kissed my temple and stood, taking my hand. "I think you should have one of us with you for a while if you plan on hanging around with him."

The logical part of my brain, the part that actually took the time to think things through all the way, knew he had a point. I wasn't about to admit that to him though. Mainly because that would give his alpha complex even more of a boost.

"Are you going to be nice? I'm not as worried about Asher and Olly." I followed him to the door where we stopped.

"I'll try my best." That was a non-answer if I'd ever heard one.

We went back into the living area and Reve, Olly, and Asher were cleaning up the dinner mess. I turned to look over my shoulder at Tobias and give him a 'see, they can get along with him' look.

"Olly wants to go see a movie." Asher flung a dishtowel over his shoulder and turned towards us. He leaned back against the counter and I about had an orgasm from how hot he looked in my kitchen. I guess a man doing the dishes was a turn on.

Naked dishes would be even better.

"I don't do well in crowds." Reve put the last dish in the dishwasher and shut it.

"You two should go." I looked between Olly and Asher. They both looked at each other before Asher shrugged his shoulders and put the dishtowel on the counter.

"I know what you're doing Dani." Asher pulled me into a hug and put his lips near my ear so only I could hear his words. "And thank you."

He pulled back and kissed me before heading to the door, Olly doing the same.

After the door clicked shut, the tension between Reve and Tobias was palpable. It was tempting to send them both on their way, but instead, I plopped down on the center cushion of the couch and patted the cushions on each side of me.

"Mind if I check the game? Then we can watch a movie or something." Tobias grabbed the remote, not waiting for my answer, and turned on the television. I didn't know much about baseball, but what I did know bored me to tears.

Reve sat down and put his arm across the back of the couch, purposely brushing his fingers against my neck. I shivered and my nipples hardened. It was the first time he'd touched me outside of a dream.

"Please don't tell me you're a Dodger's fan," Reve groaned as soon as the game was on. "No wonder you have a stick up your ass."

He twirled the end of my ponytail in his fingers as he shook his head at the screen showing the Dodgers up two runs against the Nationals. They were in the top of the eighth inning and the bases were loaded with red jerseys. I had picked up a few things about baseball from Tobias but was no expert.

"We only root for the Dodger's in this harem," Tobias said, not looking away from the television. He was leaning forward with his forearms on his legs.

I snorted. "You're the only one who watches baseball. I thought you were just checking the score."

"He's nervous, the bases are loaded." Reve was watching the screen now too.

I got bored quickly and leaned into Reve, fitting like a puzzle piece in the crook of his arm. His light touches on my skin as he played with my hair were so relaxing I felt my eyes grow heavy.

My head jerked as Reve started laughing and Tobias let out a slew of curses. Someone hit a homerun with the bases loaded.

"The Giants will always be superior to the Dodgers, by the way."

"Funny. Dodgers are at the top of the league right now. Where are the Giants? Oh, that's right, near the bottom."

I didn't know much about team rivalries in sports, but living in California for your entire life, it is well known that Dodgers fans and Giants fans did not see eye to eye.

"Can you two please stop. There's only so much of this back and forth I can take." I put my head on Reve's shoulder as Tobias looked over at me with a frown on his face.

"If he tells me he's a Raider's fan, I don't think I can deal. Raider's fans are crazy." Was he being serious? I didn't understand the obsessive nature of liking a sports team. Maybe there was a sports demon that had hold of Tobias's brain.

"Raider Nation, baby."

"You two have a lot in common after all. Both of you are sports fans and you both love me." I leaned over and grabbed the controller that Tobias was still gripping. "And you both want to make me happy by turning to something else."

"I think maybe it's time for Tobias to head home for the night."

"I'm going nowhere if you're still here."

"So, what you're saying is that if I wanted to have sex with Danica this evening, you'd want to supervise?"

"You aren't having sex with her."

"Shouldn't that be her decision? You have all had sex with her. Two of you at a time. Watching each other. Why can't I have sex with her?"

"Guys, I'm sitting right here." I couldn't believe they were still at each other's throats. Was this how parents felt when their two children bickered with each other?

"You're probably into all kinds of BDSM shit. That's not Danica's style."

"I can assure you that shit is never part of the equation. Maybe Danica has some secret fantasies you are unaware of. Did you ever think of that?"

"Like what?"

My face must have been fifty shades of red when both men turned their heads to look at me.

"Danica?" Tobias raised his eyebrows.

"I might be a little interested in trying some things out. You always threaten to spank me and you haven't yet. Being tied up appeals to me." I bit my lip because I didn't want to sound like I was unsatisfied with the sex because, hell yes, I was very satisfied. "And I definitely would be turned on if I could boss Olly and Asher around with each other."

"See? I know her better than you think." A cocky grin spread across Reve's face.

"Only because you hijacked her dreams. We

could tie you up and torture you a bit. That sounds right up your alley."

The smile slid from Reve's face and he cleared his throat before turning his attention back to me. "I should get going. I have nightmares to create."

He stood and I jumped up after him as he started walking away. I grabbed his wrist and he froze. I let go quickly.

"Reve-"

"It's fine."

I followed him to the door. Once he stepped outside, he turned towards me and gave me a small reassuring smile. It wasn't very reassuring at all.

My eyes dropped to the chain tattoo around his neck then down to the chains on his wrists. I looked back at his face.

"It was a long time ago, I just haven't been reminded of it in a while. I really do need to get to work." He put his hands in his pockets and I heard a set of keys move.

"Will you be visiting me tonight? It's been a while." I bit my lip. I missed him taking me out of my own nightmares.

"I will." Then he turned and unlocked the door to the apartment right next door.

I should have been shocked or upset with the fact that he was a level ten stalker by a human's standards, but I wasn't. I was starting to come to terms with the fact that nothing in my life was quite human anymore.

Chapter Eleven

*M*onday mornings were such a drag, but first thing when I opened my door to leave, I found another bouquet of roses sitting on my doorstep. Reve might be a demon, but he certainly was a charmer.

I quickly unwrapped the cellophane and cut off the ends. I ended up poking myself about a dozen times and wondered why floral shops didn't take more care to cut off the thorns. I emptied the packet of flower preserver in water and stuck the roses in a vase.

I drove to school and walked into class excited for once. There were only two more days of classes before three days of finals. Half of my excitement was from classes being done and half was from not having to wear the atrocious sailor's uniform anymore. Every time I looked in the mirror I thought about how easy it would be to sneak on a yacht and steal it without looking suspicious.

If I didn't need them for next year, I'd have burned them. I *really* wanted to burn them. The temptation to not return was strong.

I put my bag down on the table and approached Tobias's desk where he was staring at his computer screen with an intensity that made him sexier than usual.

"Good morning, Mr. Armstrong. How are you this marvelous Monday?"

He grunted without looking up from his computer screen. I stood there for another moment, hoping he was just in the middle of reading an email, but then he closed his computer and shuffled some papers.

I swear sometimes Tobias had mood swings like he was the one that had to deal with a bleeding vagina. Yesterday we had all, with the exception of Reve, hung out all day. Tobias even helped me study.

"You need to take a seat Ms. Deville." He looked up at me, his eyes pleading.

I tilted my head a bit, trying to figure him out. He hadn't called me Ms. Deville in what felt like forever. It was a warning.

I rolled my eyes at him and sat down in my seat just as other students began trickling in. They were talking in hushed whispers and kept sneaking glances in Tobias's direction. I picked up bits and pieces of the conversation and my eyes widened and my gut clenched.

"She moved off campus."

"He was on call Saturday night and Sunday, but he wasn't here."

"I heard Dean Whittaker got a report that our wards were compromised for a short time because he wasn't here when he was supposed to be."

"Oliver is never around anymore either."

"She must have them under some kind of spell. Do you think they even know?"

"I hope he doesn't get fired. He's my favorite teacher."

The sudden urge to vomit hit me and I tried to busy myself by getting out my notebook. This was my fault. I was the one who moved off campus. I was the one who had a demon love interest that made Tobias uncomfortable enough to shirk his duties.

I braved a glance up in Tobias's direction. He was holding it together pretty well considering what was being said about him. Well, besides the slight tremor in his hands and the frown on his face.

When Olly entered the room, the whispering stopped and more staring happened as he strode over to the seat next to me and sat down. Whispers started again and he turned to look around the room and then to look at me.

"What happened?" he asked under his breath.

"I'm not sure but they're whispering about us.

All of us. I think Tobias is in trouble." I worked my bottom lip between my teeth and took a calming breath, not that it helped much. "What if he gets fired?"

Olly made a noise somewhere between a grunt and a snort. "Michael assigned him here. He isn't going anywhere."

I considered his words, allowing myself to calm down a bit. "But he'll have some kind of consequence, won't he?"

"Stop worrying. You have enough on your plate. We've all made our choice to be with you. He's known that people might find out at some point." Olly put his hand on my thigh and squeezed.

Class started and Tobias went through what we would be covering over the next two days. Our final was on Friday so we would spend time reviewing the most important takeaways from the semester.

I tried to pay attention to his words, but my mind had other ideas and instead played through the events from the weekend. Tobias had built himself as a well-respected and competent instructor, and here I was ruining it for him.

CLASSES WERE over for the day. I was glad I no longer had to study for my GED or meet Olly to review the absurd amount of expectations at the academy. I had passed both the GED test and the bullshit made-up test with flying colors.

I walked across campus to the faculty building and let myself in. Tobias hadn't taken my keys yet. I made my way to his room and let myself in with the key he had given me. He wasn't back yet, so I planted myself on his futon.

I pulled my phone out of my bag and was surprised to see a text from my dad. He had been fairly silent lately and we hadn't been talking much. He knew I had moved, had been opposed to it as any father would, but he hadn't stopped me.

I would like to see your new place. Thursday evening?

Despite knowing that he hadn't wanted me to move off campus, I was excited to show him I was adulting. I knew he just worried about me being on my own, but I had Asher right upstairs and apparently Reve had slyly leased the apartment next door.

It was like the building was made for the three of us rejects. The ex-Fallen, the demon, and the freak.

I put my phone on the table and picked up a large, leather-covered photo album I had never seen before. Tobias didn't have pictures lying around. I flipped open the cover and smiled. These were probably the pictures Asher had gotten from Tobias's family and scanned into his computer.

The photos were black and white, but in a way that made them even more vibrant with life. You notice other things in black and white photos. The first several pages were of Tobias and his wife, Margie. In every picture of them, they were glued at the hip with smiles on their faces. There were pictures of their wedding day, them posing on a beach, and them in front of a house.

They were a beautiful couple. Tobias looked exactly the same with his trimmed beard, broad shoulders, and narrow waist. Margie was what I'm sure was considered a bombshell back during that time; a classic beauty. She had long blond hair, the softest eyes, and Marilyn Monroe-like curves.

I turned the pages and watched his children grow up before my eyes. He had done the same, watched them grow in photographs. It broke my heart to know he only had memories up until the time he left for war.

He had missed everything. Their first days of school, their first lost teeth, graduations, marriages. I wiped at my face to stop the tears from dripping onto the plastic protected pages.

I heard the door open behind me, but continued to look through the pictures. I wasn't sure if he'd be upset that I was looking at them, but I couldn't hide the fact that I had seen them. I had taken an intimate tour of his past life and a life that could have been.

"Hey." I heard his bag hit the kitchen table and his keys follow shortly behind. I could tell by the sounds that he was kicking his shoes off. First his left, then his right. It was always the same.

I didn't say anything and instead shut the album and placed it back on the table. I heard him let out a sigh as he walked towards me.

"I'm assuming you've heard the rumors?" He sat down next to me and reached forward to run his hand over the cover of the album.

"It's all anyone talked about today. No one seemed to care that I could hear every word they said." I fiddled with the hem of my button-down shirt, which I had untucked earlier. "Are you in trouble?"

He grabbed one of my hands to stop me from fiddling and laced his fingers through mine. His head landed on my shoulder and my heart nearly burst out of my chest.

"Michael is coming tomorrow after classes to meet with me and Sue." He ran his thumb back and forth across the length of my thumb. "I'm sorry about this morning. There was a pretty scathing email sent to me and Michael about it. You know how Whittaker is."

"I do. Maybe we should cool things off for a bit. Until you clear this mess up." The words felt wrong coming out of my mouth. I hadn't wanted to say them, but I also couldn't sit by and watch Tobias let his life spiral out of control because of me.

Especially not when I was harboring such a large secret that I was certain would change things.

His head popped up from my shoulder, and with his other hand, he grabbed my chin and turned my face towards him. His eyes searched mine.

"We're not running away from this. I won't run away from it." His eyes were glossy and I bit the inside of my lip, trying to keep my own tears at bay.

I nodded my head and he pulled me against him, taking the hair band out of my hair and running his fingers lightly through it.

"Don't say shit like that. It hurts." I could barely hear his voice against my hair. "I don't care what anyone says. I haven't since the moment I touched you. I love you and I'm never letting you go."

I couldn't stop the tears from falling. He said that now, but I wasn't so sure. I needed to tell them, all of them.

"Make love to me," I mumbled into his shirt.

He pulled back and looked at me, swiping his thumbs under my eyes to wipe the tears away.

"Are *you* okay?"

I nodded my response and he brushed his wet thumb over my bottom lip, my salty tears spreading over it.

"I'm fine." I shifted so I was straddling him. I really wasn't fine, and I hadn't been in a while, but telling him now would just make matters worse.

I lowered my lips to his neck and kissed my way down as I unbuttoned his shirt. Right now, what I needed was him in my mouth.

His lids grew heavy as I reached the final button and slid from his lap onto the floor in front of him. He parted his knees and I kept my eyes on his as I unbuckled his belt.

"Danica, you don't have to-" His head tilted back onto the cushion and he let out a hiss of breath as I palmed his length through his slacks.

He came to life against my hand, and despite the somber mood, I couldn't keep the smile off my face. I loved the effect I had on these men, time and time again. No matter what I said or did, they always seemed to have an eternal flame burning for me. I could only hope that it would remain.

I pulled his zipper down and tugged his pants down and off. I ran my hands up his thighs before gripping him at the base of his cock. He was fully aroused now, a bead of pre-cum already at the tip, waiting for my tongue to lap it up.

I gave him a few firm pumps before blowing air gently on the tip.

"Fucking hell." His voice was raspy with desire.

He threaded his fingers through my hair as I flicked my tongue across the head, taking a taste of him. He rolled his hips up, urging me to take him into my mouth. As much as I wanted to, I also wanted to savor him, to worship him.

I tilted my head and sucked the sensitive skin at the base, my tongue darting out to tease his balls.

His breaths became short and fast as I slowly moved my lips back to the tip and took him in my mouth. I watched his face as I took him all the way in until he hit the back of my throat.

I hummed as I worked him with my mouth, his hips moving in shallow thrusts, attempting to get deeper.

Once he was thoroughly worked up and panting, I stood up and made slow work of taking off my blazer, shirt, and skirt. He eyed me hungrily, but didn't move from his spot.

As much as he enjoyed taking charge in the bedroom, he also enjoyed torturing himself by watching. I unclasped my bra, letting it fall as I took an extra-long time sliding my panties off. I dropped them on top of his pants, the message clear. He could keep them.

I watched as he stroked himself before I lowered onto his lap, my knees on either side of him. I braced my hands on the back of the futon as he helped guide himself into me until we were completely connected.

Our lips touched in a gentle kiss that left my toes curling as I began rolling my hips. This was my favorite position, the downward movement always hitting my clit just the right way.

Tobias buried his face in my neck, sucking the skin lightly as I increased my pace. His hands slid to my ass and palmed my flesh.

"Spank me," I breathed, barely managing to get the words out as my body prepared itself to erupt. I gripped the back of the futon and felt my body tense as one of his hands moved and then sent a sharp slap to my cheek.

"Jesus, Danica," he growled, rubbing the spot. His hips began working under mine, pushing himself deeper.

"Again." I'd never been spanked before, and now I wondered why I had waited so long to request it. When his flattened palm hit my ass again, my muscles clenched around him and my orgasm hit with such force that I ceased to exist. My bones turned to jelly and I could barely move.

Taking that as his cue to take over, he lifted me and laid me on the futon, settling between my legs. I arched my body into his and brought his lips back to mine.

He moved in slow, torturous strokes with his face buried in the crook of my neck. I clung to him like he was the anchor keeping me from floating away.

As his pace increased, I felt another orgasm building deep inside of me. My skin felt feverish from the friction of our bodies and the prolonged love making that was making my head feel fuzzy.

Tobias came in a final deep thrust that sent me over the edge with him, our bodies shuddering as they rode out the waves of pleasure.

"That was..." I couldn't find the words to describe it. I loved sex, but this transcended sex. It was a declaration.

"I love you." He kissed my cheek and then

pulled back, concern in his eyes. "You're burning up."

I raised a hand to my cheek and shrugged. "Fantastic sex will do that to a person."

"I don't have a thermometer." Tobias pulled out, leaving me feeling empty, and stood. I gazed up at him. "You look really flushed."

"I'm fine." I sat up and my head spun. That was some orgasm. "Really. Don't worry so much. I'm sure in a few minutes my body will realize the orgasms are done with. At least for now."

He went into his bathroom and returned with a washcloth and folded it in fourths. He put it across my forehead. I sighed and leaned my head back to keep it from falling off.

He sat down, still naked, next to me. "Have you been sleeping at all?"

"Yes, better than I have in months thanks to Reve." I shut my eyes and let the cool washcloth work its magic. I felt Tobias's hands stroking the hair back from my face.

He made a noise in his throat and I cracked an eye open to see him staring intently at me. I shut it again and focused on the feel of his fingers smoothing back my hair.

"What if one night he decides to torment you in your dreams?"

"He won't."

"You don't know that."

I was quiet for several minutes before responding. "I do know that. Just like I know that all of you have my best interests at heart, even when you drive me nuts sometimes."

"He's a-"

I cut him off, not wanting to hear him say the five-letter word again. "I don't care. My dad is the devil. My mom is Lilith. Asher used to be Fallen. You're being close-minded and not thinking about how much he's helping me or about how much I-" I opened my eyes and stared at the ceiling fan. There was something soothing about watching the blades spin. "How much I love him. I haven't been doing well, Tobias. You know it. I know it. Everyone knows it. Let me have the peace he brings me, please."

I sounded desperate. I *was* desperate. I hated feeling like my life was spiraling out of control. For once I wanted to be in control of my own destiny, even if that meant pissing off some people along the way.

"Okay."

"Okay?" I cocked an eyebrow and the washcloth slid off and plopped onto my chest. Tobias ran his fingers over my moist forehead. "Just like that you're okay with me and Reve?"

"Just like that." He placed his lips against my cheek. "I love you. If you think Reve will help you in a way we can't... I don't want you to resent me."

I brought my hand to his cheek. "I could never resent you. I love you."

"The biggest issue is he likes the Giants *and* the Raiders. It's completely unacceptable. I don't see how it's going to work."

I groaned and couldn't keep the smile from spreading across my face.

Chapter Twelve

I could taste the sweet flavors of freedom. One more final left on Friday and I was home free, or at least academy free for the summer. Well, besides the independent study classes I had to complete from semester one.

I sat with my feet propped on my ottoman and stared at the blank television screen. I didn't need to study for my Demonology final so I was left with nothing to do but wait for my dad to show up.

I hadn't seen him since I told him we dug up Lily's grave and had barely spoken to him. He was preoccupied, and I couldn't blame him. I didn't even want to imagine what he was going through.

First he finds out his partner was lying to him, then that his daughter is half demon, and then to top it all off, that the casket was empty. It was a lot for me to handle with the support of my angels. He was dealing with the shitstorm alone.

I knew I needed to tell my angels I was half demon. The thing was, I didn't feel like a demon, not that I would know what that felt like. I didn't feel like an angel either though.

I must have fallen asleep on the couch because I was jolted awake by a sharp knock on the door. I rubbed my eyes and went to the door.

I opened it, finding my father standing outside, dressed in a charcoal gray suit. He looked tired. He never looked tired. I moved out of the way for him to enter and shut the door.

"Dad," I greeted him, standing there awkwardly. The last time we had been in the same room with each other he had told me to get out.

"Give me a tour?" He walked into the kitchen and I followed, biting my lip. I guess he was still upset. He looked around, but didn't say another word.

"Well, obviously this is the kitchen. That's the living room." He followed me, nodding his head in what I hoped was approval until we got to the bedroom. "The bedroom."

I stepped inside and did a sweeping motion with my hand. His eyebrows nearly shot off his face as he took in the bed that nearly took up the entire space.

"Danica Marie. What in the hell do you need a bed this big for?" He must have realized he didn't really want the answer to that question. "Never mind. Some things fathers don't need to know."

He followed me back into the living room and we sat on the couch. Several awkward moments of silence passed before we both started talking at once.

"I'm sorry I dug up Mom's grave."

"I shouldn't have snapped like I did."

He ran a hand over his face before continuing. "You shouldn't be prying into this, Danica. Clearly she is up to something if she felt the need to have a child then fake her own death. Then almost two decades later start abducting angels for their blood."

"Are you sure it's her?" I asked in a whisper.

"We're positive it's her. She was here and we think she's been following you. Michael was able to get the security footage from the grocery store. She looks different than she did eighteen years ago." He cleared his throat. "We think she and John are in Shanghai, China, right now. There have been angel disappearances there. We just can't figure out what role John plays in all of this, unless he's under her spell."

"She can put a spell on people?" I drew my eyebrows together, considering his words. I was fairly certain the woman behind me in the bathroom line at Universal Studios had been her too. What other explanation was there for her disappearing suddenly and the woman behind me saying there had been no one?

"She is certainly manipulative. With humans she might be able to sway their thoughts. I honestly don't know what she's capable of. If she's capable of having a child and then faking her own death, well..." He adjusted the watch on his wrist. I had never seen him so antsy in my life.

"I haven't told the guys about what this all means for me." I tried to keep the tears that were filling my eyes from spilling over, but a few escaped and trailed down my cheeks.

He scooted over on the couch and pulled me into a hug. "It doesn't mean anything. You're the same girl you were before we knew she was Lilith."

I shook my head and let the tears soak his suit jacket. "I don't know who I am anymore."

He rubbed my back in small circles and I felt the tension leaving my shoulders. I hadn't even realized they'd been so tense.

"You need to tell them. You shouldn't have to carry the weight of this on your shoulders. They love you. They know that your blood isn't what defines you."

"But it does. They-" I stopped short, realizing he didn't know about Reve. Their reactions to Reve said enough about what their reaction to me would be.

"They what?" He pulled back and looked at me, worry plaguing his face.

"They don't like demons."

"They've never even met a demon. And you're forgetting something very important. You aren't a demon." He brushed the tears from my cheeks.

"I'm not an angel either then. So what am I, Dad? Just a freak?"

He took a sharp inhale of breath and searched my eyes like he was seeing me for the first time. Seeing the woman who was confused about who she was and what that meant.

"You're-"

"Danica, you home?" Reve's head came through the brick wall separating his apartment from mine. He really had the worst timing.

When his eyes landed on Lucifer they went wide and I could tell he tried to retreat but something in the air shifted. He was frozen in place, stuck with his head through the wall.

"Sir," Reve said in a strangled voice. "I can't breathe."

Lucifer stood and walked over to the wall where Reve was trapped. I stood too, but stayed where I was. I could feel the air pulsating with the threat of violence.

"Reve." His voice was rough and angry. He grabbed a handful of Reve's hair and yanked him through the wall the rest of the way before slamming him up against the brick so hard the mounted television shook.

"Sir, I can explain." Lucifer's hand was around his throat, Reve's feet hanging a foot above the ground.

"How do you know Danica?"

A choking sound came from Reve and his face

turned bright red. He was trying to speak but Lucifer's grip was crushing his throat.

"Dad. Stop." I was frozen in place, watching the train that was my life speed down the mountain, ready to wreck.

He turned his head towards me and his face made me back up a step. He was barely containing his anger and I knew if I didn't calm him down, it would be a repeat of when I told him about Lily's grave.

"He's... I'm in love with him." My voice was shaking as I said the words and his head snapped back around to look at Reve.

"How is she in love with a demon whose sole purpose on this Earth is to punish people with nightmares?" Reve's feet kicked against the wall as he struggled to get air. "Are you what's been causing her to lose sleep?"

He shook his head vigorously, his eyes wide.

Finally, my feet started working and I rushed to them. I grabbed the arm that was holding Reve hostage.

This was why I was scared to tell Tobias, Asher, and Olly I was a demon. Even my own father wasn't immune to the disgust towards them. I could see it in his eyes.

I choked on a sob and yanked his arm again. He relented and dropped Reve who took such a large gasp of air, I thought he might suck all of the air out of the room.

"How can you say that me having demon blood means nothing when you... when you..." I couldn't get the words out so instead I just punched him in the arm in frustration. I might as well have punched the brick wall.

He grabbed my fist as I was about to punch him again. "You know that's not-"

"It *is* the same thing!" I yelled, and tried to yank my arm away. "Where does this leave me? I'm not angel enough to be an angel, I have no wings, my mother is some kind of demon, and now my father is looking at me like he doesn't even know me." I managed to get my arm free and turned away from the two men who were staring at me with what looked very much like pity. "My own mother didn't even want me."

I was spiraling. I knew that. I was never one for self-loathing, but that was until the world seemed out to take me down. Other eighteen-year olds didn't have to wonder if they were going to suddenly sprout ten heads or tentacles. With my luck, I'd morph into a fingernail demon and be condemned to a life of munching on fingernails.

Reve appeared in front of me and I looked away.

"Look at me." His voice was raspy, probably from being almost choked to death by the devil.

I shook my head and he took my chin and forced my eyes to meet his.

"Am I evil?" I shook my head. "Then what

makes you think you are? You are the farthest from evil I have ever seen. Your heart and soul are so overflowing with love and light that you could never be evil."

"But they... does it matter how I feel?" I might not feel like anything other than a plain old human, but when people treated you differently, it made you feel like less of one.

"I think to them, it does matter how you feel. They didn't kill me. Your father hasn't killed me."

"Yet."

Reve rolled his eyes and I started to laugh. I was standing in a room with a devil and a demon who just rolled his eyes at him. Sometimes I wondered if I would one day wake up in a mental institution in a straitjacket and padded room, having imagined it all.

He pulled me towards him and wrapped his arms around me. I heard my dad grumbling and braved a look over my shoulder to see him running his fingers through his hair and shaking his head.

"Dad?" I pulled away and stepped around Reve. "What's wrong?"

"The prophecy. It's true. Of course it's true. Lucifer and Lilith, his greatest regrets have a daughter that has to save us all." He started laughing and Reve let me go. I backed up a step. "Is this my redemption?" He spread his arms out and spoke to the ceiling. "Really fucking funny! Isn't a life in hell enough?"

Reve grabbed my hand. "Sir, from what I've overheard about the prophecy, it sounds like a load of crap. It is well known in the dream demon community that Nostradamus was plagued by a rogue dream demon for many years."

"Like you're plaguing my daughter?" He turned and his eyes went straight to our connected hands. "Reve. This is-"

"I know what it seems like, Sir, but I can assure you that I've only brought happiness to Danica's dreams."

I didn't know whether to fear for him or be in awe of him for interrupting and standing up to my father. When my father looked over at me, I nodded.

"I need to contact Michael. Damn it. I'm going to have to admit that he was right." He stared at Reve for a moment. "If you hurt her, I will rescind my protection."

Protection? I opened my mouth to ask but Reve answered, "I can assure you, I won't."

With one last look, Lucifer vanished.

∼

I SENT A GROUP TEXT. *Meet me on the roof.*

I was already a mess, might as well rip the Band-Aid clean off the wound and bleed out if necessary.

Reve was by my side, holding my hand, when

Olly, Asher, and Tobias landed on the roof together. Had they all been off doing something together? I guess it made sense, since I told them my dad and I were going to hang out.

Although I'd hardly call the events downstairs hanging out.

We met in the middle of the roof and I shut my eyes for a brief moment. I was experiencing an extreme case of déjà vu from the recurring nightmare I'd been having, except this time, Reve was right next to me.

"I need to talk to you all about something." Reve gave my hand a reassuring squeeze as I spoke. Three sets of eyes tracked his movements.

I looked between them before letting go of Reve's hand. I moved to stand in front of each of them, looking them in the eye one by one. I needed to tell them.

What do I say? How do I say it?

My breathing felt irregular as I stopped in front of Olly. If anyone was going to accept the fact that I was of diabolical origins, it was him.

"Dani?" Olly's voice was laced with concern.

"My mother, Lily, is Lilith. She is a demon." I shut my eyes and let the setting sun hit my face, the warmth doing nothing to ease the chill that had come over me. "I'm not half human. I'm part angel, part demon."

Complete silence fell on the roof, it seemed even the traffic and noise on the street below had been muted for this moment. My words sounded completely crazy, even to my own ears.

"I figured as much," Tobias said.

"Me too," Asher confirmed.

I looked at Olly who was staring at me, hurt in his eyes. It was a look that wasn't common on his face and it broke my heart.

"You've known this since Spring break?" I nodded in reply. "And you kept it from us?"

I reached forward to grab his hand but he backed up a step. "Olly, I was-"

"You were what, Danica? Scared of how we'd react? Scared we would up and leave?" Both Asher and Tobias stood with wide eyes as Olly showed an emotion we hadn't seen before: anger. "I can't be here right now."

Before anyone could say anything to stop him, his wings extended and he shot into the sky like a blur.

"I'm going to go after him," Asher said. He cupped my cheek and then followed Olly.

I brought one of my hands to my mouth to contain the sob that was threatening to spill out. Tobias stepped forward and wrapped his arms around me.

"He'll come around. He's just been really worried about you these past few weeks. I think he knew too, but you just hadn't confirmed it." He kissed my temple and then looked over at Reve who was standing back, observing.

"I'm not going anywhere," Reve said.

Tobias sighed and walked over to stand in front of him. "We're not going anywhere either."

"So where does that leave us, angel? I don't intend to hurt anyone. If I do, Lucifer will have my head." Reve stuck out his hand. "Truce?"

Tobias eyed his hand and finally took it, the two shaking.

MY HAND SHOOK SLIGHTLY as I stared down at the unopened text message from Olly. Out of the three, I never expected him to be as upset as he was.

Tobias and Reve were oblivious to the world. They had somehow managed to settle on watching a baseball game and wanted the same team to win. I was glad for the time being they were at least making an attempt to get along.

I finally clicked the text open. *I'm sorry I flew off like that. It's not because you have demon blood, it's because you kept it from us and were suffering because of it. I'll see you tomorrow for our final.*

I let out a shaky breath of air and Tobias's and Reve's heads turned towards me.

"Olly texted me. Everything's fine, I think." I slumped down in the chair and put my head on the cushion. "I should come with the warning label 'requires patience.'"

Tobias snorted.

"Am I missing something?" Reve asked.

"Just as she said. She sometimes requires patience. I'm working on having more of it myself," Tobias answered with a chuckle.

"I've been getting a little better. Making a conscious effort," I defended myself. Unfortunately, I could think of several things in the past month where a little more thought would have been advantageous.

"It makes things interesting. I think we all should be a little more spur of the moment."

I heard the television go silent and then movement. I popped open an eye to see Tobias standing next to the chair. He had a look in his eye.

"I have *your* final tomorrow," I warned, sitting up all the way and glancing at Reve who appeared to be in deep thought. "Stop looking at me like that."

"How am I looking at you?" A smirk formed on his face as he grabbed me and threw me over his shoulder.

I reached down and swatted his ass. "Put me down. We should be going to sleep soon."

"It's barely nine. If anyone should be worried about what time they're going to be sleeping, it's Reve since he's ancient." Tobias smoothed a hand over my ass and walked towards the bedroom.

I lifted my head to look to Reve for help but he just stood and followed silently.

"Reve, aren't you going to say anything back to that? He just called you an old man."

Reve looked directly in my eyes and slowly shook his head.

His lack of words was making my heartbeat go straight to my clit. Tobias dumped me on the bed and lay down next to me. I made a move to roll towards him but he pinned my wrists as he moved to hover over me.

"Tobias, what do you think you're doing?" I looked up at him and licked my lips, ready for him to come in for the kill.

"I'm being spur of the moment. Plus keeping your mind occupied. You've been thinking too much lately." He let go of one of my wrists and trailed a finger down my cheek, causing me to shiver with pleasure. He lowered his lips to my ear. "The whole time, I'll be watching to make sure he behaves himself."

He wasn't even touching me and I felt a jolt of electricity between my legs. He pushed up off the bed and I looked past him, but Reve was nowhere to be seen. Had I missed how this had even transpired?

"He left!" I sat up on my forearms. "Maybe he's not into-"

"I'm into it." I heard his voice next to me on the bed and turned.

Tobias let me go and sat on the other side of the

bed. I turned back to the direction Reve's voice had come from.

"Show yourself." My heart was thudding in my chest as I watched his hand appear and move towards the hem of my shirt. "Reve, what are you doing?"

"Am I scaring you?" His voice was like a caress.

"No, but-" His finger came to my lip to hush me. He ran it along my bottom lip before trailing it down to lift my shirt off. "You didn't hear a thing Tobias and I talked about while you stared at your phone, did you?"

"Well, no. Weren't you talking about RBIs and pinch hitters? Hardly anything I want to listen to." His finger appeared and traced along the edge of my bra before disappearing again. It was like being blind-folded, but not. My breath came in small gasps as his fingers touched my skin and then disappeared again.

"I told him I was going to have sex with you and asked him if he had a problem with that."

"And what did he say?" I breathed as his hand unclasped my bra and pulled it off.

His mouth appeared above my breast and he swirled his tongue around the rosy bud that was so hard it almost hurt. I arched off the bed and tried to grab him but he disappeared.

"Can't try to touch me when I'm doing this." He ran a finger down my stomach to my pants and unbuttoned them.

"Tobias said he still didn't trust me, but that if you wanted this then he was going to have to be fine with it. But he wants to watch." He put his mouth next to my ear. "Do you want him to watch? Because I don't mind. Maybe he'll learn a thing or two."

I let out a moan that was answer enough and Reve reappeared, completely naked. He was exactly as he was in my dreams; muscled and tattooed from his neck to his feet. He was magnificent.

He wasted no time removing my pants and panties. He sat back on his heels and stared down at me with hooded eyes before a wicked grin spread across his face. Then he faded from sight.

I looked over at Tobias, who hadn't moved from the other end of the bed, but was watching intently. I always thought it would be weird to have someone watch me have sex, but since these men came into my life, it was nothing but a turn-on. The self-control it must have taken to just sit back and watch was something I couldn't do. I had struggled just watching Asher and Olly kiss.

He rubbed a palm over his erection through his pants. I felt lips on my inner thigh and gripped the sheets to avoid trying to grab at Reve.

"Holy shit." The lips moved up and brushed along the outer folds of my pussy. It was killing me not being able to see him or anticipate what he was going to do next. "Reve, please."

I don't know what I was begging for, but I was

begging for *something*. A finger ran along my slit, spreading my slickness with it. It wasn't something new I had never experienced before, but when you couldn't see anything that was happening but could still *see*, it was something else entirely.

"Oh my God. Are you going to fuck me while you're like this?" The thought made me jack my hips towards him. "Reve!" Two fingers thrust into me and I heard Tobias chuckle.

I turned my head towards him and watched as he stroked himself, his cock pulled free of his pants. I bit my lip and he tightened his fist.

"I've never heard you so vocal." His voice was low and he groaned as Reve appeared again and met my lips.

"If this makes you uncomfortable, I'll stop." Reve slid his erection along my pussy and put the tip at my entrance.

"It doesn't." I traced his cheek with my finger and then he vanished again and then thrust into me in one smooth move. "Oh, God damn."

My voice seemed to fail me as he thrust in and out of me with such even and smooth thrusts that I wondered if he was some kind of sex robot. I could hear his grunts and breaths, but not seeing him was driving me crazy and we'd barely even started.

"I'm going to come," I said through clenched teeth. "Reve!" His name left me in a rush as my orgasm shook my body.

Reve reappeared and I dug my nails into his

back. He groaned and pulled me to my hands and knees, facing Tobias who was working his cock with such force, I thought he might break it off.

He thrust back into me from behind and pulled me back against him, one arm going across my chest, holding me in place, and the other going to my clit and matching Tobias's speed.

A chorus of "fucks" filled the room as we all fell head first into orgasms. I fell onto the bed, still convulsing with pleasure as Reve pulled me to his chest and lay behind me.

And to think I had wondered how I'd ever please four men.

Chapter Thirteen

My last final was Demonology. I was more than ready to ace it, but of course I woke up with a splitting headache. I stopped on the way to campus and got a Diet Dr. Pepper, hoping it would help.

When I had first quit soda cold turkey, I had gotten similar headaches that had taken me a solid week to shake. I was probably just stressed or stayed up too late with Tobias and Reve.

I made my way across campus, the bright morning sun making me shield my eyes with my hand. I loved the sun, but today I wanted it to hide behind some clouds.

I trudged my way up the two flights of stairs, feeling my pulse behind my eyes with each step I took. If an archangel could heal bruises, maybe they could also heal a headache.

I took my seat next to Olly and pulled out a pen. I had barely made it in time.

"Can you heal a headache?" I glanced over at Olly, who was folding a piece of paper into an intricate design.

He didn't look up from his paper folding. "I don't know. Let me finish this and I'll try."

"Settle down and we'll get started," Tobias said, standing from his desk with a stack of booklets in his hand. "It's been a pleasure teaching you this semester. Good luck and have a great summer."

"I bet he did have a lot of pleasure this semester," I heard someone mumble a few rows back. Several students snickered and Tobias cleared his throat.

While he was passing out our finals, I felt Oliver slide his hand into the pocket of my blazer. I looked at the two of him and then rubbed my eyes. Jesus, I had never seen double before, not even high or drunk.

"Read that later." He put his cool hand on my forehead and I flinched at how cold it felt. "You're really hot."

"Uhm, thanks?" I felt a tingling sensation but nothing else. He removed his hand.

"I mean your forehead. It's burning up. Maybe you should go to the-"

"The final is out. No talking," Tobias warned.

Olly gave me a concerned look but I just shook my head and opened my booklet. I stared down at the first question. I knew my shit. I had this one in the bag. I put my name on the top and answered the first question.

The room was silent besides the soft whir of the air conditioner, pens moving across pages, and my heartbeat that seemed to be beating in my ears.

I pinched the bridge of my nose and turned the page. I rested my chin on my fist that I had placed on the table. My eyes felt like they were about to pop out of my head and my vision blurred again.

Crap. Was this what a migraine felt like? I'd never had one, but this was far more than any headache. I stood abruptly as nausea surged in my belly. It felt like the room was spinning. My stomach felt like it was stuck in the spin cycle of the washing machine.

"Danica?" I wasn't sure who said it; the voice was hard to make out behind the ringing in my ears.

I stumbled out from behind the table and headed for the door. I needed air. I needed to get outside. I felt warm liquid on my face and reached up to wipe at it. I pulled my hand away and stared down at the bright red liquid. I quickly put my hand back up to cup my nose.

I could feel the blood oozing through my fingers. I made it to the door and lowered my hand to grip the door handle. There was so much blood; where was it all coming from? Had my brain exploded?

The classroom behind me had erupted in chatter and several chairs scraped across the floor. I couldn't hear what the voices were saying as I managed to get the door open.

I stumbled into the empty hall and fell.

A FAINT TICKING PULLED me out of the darkness that had taken me under. I wasn't dreaming. I wasn't having a nightmare. It was just an emptiness staring back at me, black and infinite.

My eyelids felt heavy, and after several attempts at opening them, I gave up. Instead, I tapped into my other senses that did seem to be working. My skin felt clammy and cold, goosebumps slowly moving across my skin as my body registered that it was cold in the room. What the fuck had happened to me?

I heard voices behind a closed door drawing nearer. The sound of a door opening.

"How is she?" It was Tobias.

"We think we have the fever and bleeding under control," my dad responded. His voice had an edge to it.

"What are you doing here?" Tobias said, not sounding happy at all. It was hard to see who he was talking to. My eyes seemed to be stuck shut.

"I called him," Olly said. "He is just as much a part of this as we are."

Tobias made a noise in his throat. "A part of this? Ever since he's been around she's been a mess. Can't sleep, her focus is even worse, and now she's sick. Interesting it happened right after she slept with him."

"Tobias," Asher warned.

"Did you ever stop to consider that *you* three are the cause of this? Her nightmares only have you in them. When Asher died, it changed her. Plus, you have stressed her out beyond belief because I'm a demon." I heard several footsteps and then Reve warned, "Get your hand off me, angel."

"Stop." My voice sounded foreign in my ears, like it was laced with gravel. I managed to pry my eyes open just a fraction, enough that when the light seeped in, I clenched them shut again.

A hand took mine. "Danica, sweetie. How are you feeling?" My dad put two hands around mine. They were cold against my skin. "She has a fever again. Damn it. Where are they?"

Where was who? Where was I?

"Folks, let's clear the room so we can check her vitals," a male voice I didn't recognize said. "Lucifer can stay. Maybe you four can try to find out where Michael is and the ETA for Raphael."

I heard grumbles and feet retreating before the door was shut.

"Danica? I'm Dr. Hughes and this is my assistant, Diane. Can you open your eyes for me?"

"Bright." I managed to say. My throat and

mouth felt like the Sahara desert. I needed water. Stat.

I heard a lamp switch being turned and slowly opened my eyes. It wasn't as bright as before. The overhead light was turned off and a bedside lamp was switched on. I looked around. I was in my own room, on my giant bed.

"Very good. How is your head feeling? Oliver said you complained of a headache before passing out."

I looked at the doctor who was dressed in normal street clothes and his assistant who was dressed similarly. Then I turned my head to see my father standing a few feet back, his brows furrowed in worry. He was wearing part of his normal attire. Not only was his hair a mess, but his jacket and tie were missing. The top two buttons of his shirt were unbuttoned and the hem was untucked. He looked about as good as I felt.

"Water." I could tell my throat was only going to handle one-word answers until I had some water. I was parched.

Lucifer went over to a chair that had been dragged into the room from the kitchen table and grabbed a water bottle off the floor. The doctor and his assistant moved out of the way and he sat on the side of the bed. He put his arm under me, helping me to sit up halfway.

I winced, my muscles not liking the movement, and stopped once I was elevated enough not to choke. I took the bottle in my hands and he helped me raise it to my lips. The cool liquid slid down my throat and I felt immediate relief.

He helped me lie back down and put the bottle on the nightstand. He stayed next to me and took my hand, his own shaking slightly.

"I feel funny." I didn't quite know how to describe how I felt. I didn't feel like I had my own body. Almost like my brain had been transplanted into someone else.

The doctor crossed his arms and then brought one of his hands to his chin in thought. "Your blood sample seems to indicate some kind of autoimmune response. We were unable to pinpoint the exact cause. Mr. Armstrong mentioned you had inter-course last night with a demon?"

Well, now my body felt like it was back. My face heated up and I avoided looking at my dad. Instead, I looked down at where he held my hand, stroking it with his thumb.

"I don't see how that has anything to do with this." My voice shook as I spoke.

"Danica, this is important." I looked up at my dad; his eyes were pleading.

I sighed and let my head sink farther into the pillow. "I did."

"Was anything abnormal? Did you use protec-tion?" The doctor sounded so clinical. I wondered if he was an angel or just a regular person that somehow was privy to angels and demons.

"No. I have a birth control implant. There was nothing abnormal about it. It was better than usual." I thought back to last night. The details were a little fuzzy at the moment, but the way he had touched me had been far from abnormal.

My heart stopped as my brain played through last night. The mirror. My eyes. "My eyes."

"What about your eyes?"

"When we were done, I went into the bathroom to clean up and my eyes were weird. The pupils were so dilated that the iris color was practically gone. I splashed water on my face and they were normal again. I thought it was just from, you know... the orgasms."

My dad made a strangled noise and I wanted to go back to the black void I had been asleep in.

"Besides intercourse, was there anything else abnormal you did last night? Anything new you ate or drank?"

"I had a glass of wine." I shrugged. If it was the wine, then damn, this was some hangover.

"Thank you. We'll let you rest now and be back in later to check on you." The doctor and assistant left the room.

"Dad, you don't think this is from sleeping with Reve, do you? What even happened?"

"I'm not sure what to think." He ran his free hand through his hair. "You passed out in the hall at the academy. Your nose was bleeding so badly the blood was also coming out of your mouth. They were going to take you to a human hospital but your temperature reached one hundred and ten degrees."

A tear escaped his eye and he wiped it away. I'd never seen him shed a tear in my entire life.

"Shouldn't I be dead?" I whispered. "Why am I not dead?"

"I don't know. Both Oliver and I tried healing you, but it only seems to help for a bit before your fever spikes again. We're trying to get in contact with Raphael. He's the best healer there is."

There was a soft knock on the door and Olly entered the room. He looked tired with dark circles under his eyes.

"Michael says that Raphael is in the Congo dealing with an Ebola outbreak. He's having trouble getting into contact with him." He sat down in the chair at the end of the bed. "He's headed there now to find him."

A cell phone buzzed and my dad stood and walked around to the other side of the bed where his jacket and tie were. He dug his phone out of the pocket and looked at the screen before cursing under his breath and answering.

"This better be an emergency... Now is not the time for jokes... How?... What do you mean you don't know how?... I'm the only one who can open it... That's impossible!... Where?" He jammed his finger onto the screen and I could see the tension in his shoulders and the deep breaths he was taking.

"What's wrong?" Olly was brave asking when he was clearly trying to calm down.

My dad turned and looked at me then at Olly. "Demons got through." He held up his hand when Olly's mouth opened to speak. "I don't know how. It's an impossibility. The only demons that can go through the gate are the ones I personally escort."

I blinked several times, trying to process the information. Demons were through the gate? What did that even mean?

Olly hopped to his feet. "We need to call Michael."

"Michael needs to find Raphael. We'll go."

"Dad? What's happening?" I was confused. Maybe it was partly the fever's fault, or partly just because I missed parts of the conversation.

"Danica, we have to take care of this before they terrorize Los Angeles. There's at least half a dozen. We'll be back. Dr. Hughes and Diane will be here. They're both angels." He leaned down and kissed my forehead, the gesture bringing tears to my eyes.

Somehow, over the past several months, instead of growing further apart than we already had been, we had become closer. Sure, I always had a decent relationship with him, but since losing my shit when Asher died, he had become increasingly present. I didn't want him to leave my side. I felt a little like a five-year old that wanted her daddy when she was sick.

"Get some rest. We'll be back before you wake up." Olly gave me a small smile and followed my dad out of the room.

I let my tears fall. My cheeks felt warm to the touch as I wiped them away. I pulled the covers up around me and shut my eyes.

I'M NOT sure how long I slept, but I felt a presence in the room as I came out of a foggy, dreamless sleep. My eyes opened much easier this time and landed on a woman sitting in a chair next to my bed.

As my eyes focused, I took in a sharp breath. It was her.

It was the woman from the grocery store. She was still dressed to the nines. She stared back at me as our eyes met. In the grocery store, hers had been blue, but in hindsight they had been so blue that they had to have been contacts.

"You're awake."

I just blinked back at her, trying to make sense of her black eyes. The entire iris was black. They were larger than normal irises, but still had the white surrounding them.

I brought a shaking hand to my mouth as everything started to click together. The sunglasses perched on her head. The eyes. The hair that was the same shade of brown as mine. The nose.

"You." It was the only word I could manage. I squinted, trying to imagine her with a scarf around her head. I had only caught a glimpse. But those heels. That voice. It all came rushing back.

"Me." She reached forward and tried to take the hand lying at my side but I pulled it onto my chest. I clutched the blanket to me.

She let out a small laugh. "I don't blame you." She stood and walked to the end of the bed and then back to the chair. She sat down, crossed her legs, moved her leg a few times, then stood again.

A tear slid down my cheek. Now was not the time to cry. But God damn it, this had to be Lily, Lilith, my mother. I wasn't sure what to label her. I took in several deep breaths. Where was my dad? My guardians?

"Are you scared of your own mother?"

It had seemed like an eternity since I had been awake. My eyes felt heavy.

I couldn't find words so I just stared back at her. Stared at how similar we were. I gripped the blanket tighter.

"You have no reason to be scared." She sat again and leaned forward. "I'm the one who's going to save you."

"You abandoned me." I stared back at her, even though her eyes were freaking me out. I wouldn't let this woman intimidate me. "I'll take my chances with the angels."

She laughed again and leaned back in the chair.

She stared at me for several moments and then her face softened and she almost appeared to not look like a psychopath.

"Leaving you behind was one of the hardest things I ever had to do."

I narrowed my eyes and made a disbelieving noise in my throat. "Is that why you kidnapped me and put me in a cage? Is that why you're here now?" My teeth chattered as I spoke.

I was sure my fever was spiking again. Where had the doctor and his assistant gone? How did Lilith even get into my place?

"You were an added bonus to snagging the archangel. John only put you in the basement because he wasn't sure what was going to happen to you. You are the first of your kind, after all." She stood. She certainly was antsy, like she had bottled energy trying to escape. "Your fever is increasing again and your angels are currently occupied dealing with my soldiers. They won't return for a while, if they return at all. The choice is yours."

"How did you..." I shook my head, not believing a word from her lips.

"You do know the 'gate' just refers to the ability to pass through the barrier between Earth and Inferna, don't you?" I shook my head. What was I supposed to think? A gate is a fucking gate. "Let's just say that I have figured out how to get demons through. Now," her voice lilted higher in excitement. "We need to leave."

"I'm not going anywhere with you."

"You can stay here and always be mediocre, or you can join me and become the queen you are." Queen? Was this woman on something? It was possible she was tripping out on something.

"I have everything I need here."

"You don't need them. Why do you think four men are in love with you?" I couldn't stop my face from displaying my shock at her words. "It's in your blood. It's the same way I sucked your father in. The same way I sucked John in. You can have as many men or women as your heart and body desires."

I shifted in the bed, my muscles protesting at the small movement. "I'd rather die."

A phone rang from a leather handbag sitting next to the chair. Her grin broadened and she reached inside it and pulled out her cell phone.

"Perfect timing." She pressed a button on the screen and held it away from her to video chat. "Are your tasks complete?"

"They are. I sent four of my best to meet up with the others with enough demon serum to take down an army of angels. I'm also ready to move in on the girl at your command, my queen." The voice was gruff.

"Let us see the girl." Lilith waited for a moment before turning the phone towards me.

It was a dark blur of people and blue lights before whoever was holding the phone adjusted the angle and it was pointing at a large tank behind a bar. Inside were women with mermaid tails and shockingly blue hair.

"Don't," I managed to choke out, a sob lodged in my throat.

"I'll call off my men if you come with me. Otherwise, I'm afraid there's nothing that will help them."

I shut my eyes. I didn't have a choice. I couldn't just let everyone I loved die or be gravely injured. "Call them off and I'll go."

"You heard the girl. Stay on standby though, just in case she tries anything," she said into the phone before hanging up. What would I try? I was sick and could barely throw a punch. "Get dressed. I will wait for you in the living room."

She exited the room, leaving the door open behind her. I slid from the bed, and on shaky legs, changed out of the pajamas I was in. I pulled on a pair of loose jeans and a t-shirt. I spotted my blazer in a heap on the floor and picked it up, feeling the weight of my cell phone in the pocket.

I took it out and my fingers brushed a folded piece of paper. The note Olly slid in my pocket during the final stared back at me and I slipped it into my bra before tapping open my cell phone. I figured that Lilith was going to take my phone or search me at some point, so I quickly typed out a message to my dad.

It was a trap. Lilith is here. This is all my fault. I'm

sorry. I love you. Tell Tobias, Asher, Olly, and Reve that I love them too.

I hit send and then deleted the message from the thread just as Lilith came back in the room. She narrowed her eyes and snatched the phone from me. She threw it across the room, hitting the brick wall, causing it to shatter.

I flinched and she grabbed my arm, her nails digging into my skin.

"Let's go."

"But I need my shoes!" Before I could even move to grab them, she was pulling me towards the door.

As we entered the living space, my eyes immediately landed on Dr. Hughes and Diane sprawled out on the floor. I yanked my arm, but despite her petite size, she was stronger than ten men.

The front door opened and two abnormally large men stepped in and one picked me up. They looked like those men that flipped logs and pulled airplanes. Lilith went back into my apartment as I was loaded into a black SUV with limo tinting on the windows. I stopped struggling, my head hurting again. It was no use anyways.

I had made my decision to save the ones I loved.

Chapter Fourteen

Tobias

*T*he day had been a complete and utter disaster. There had been a lot of disastrous days lately. I could really go for a vacation from it all.

The night before, I watched Danica have sex with Reve. Really good sex with Reve.

Yeah, it bothered me, but watching them together turned me on. If he made her happy, it seemed I was going to have to accept it or, well, I wasn't sure what other choice I had. She was headstrong about what she wanted.

The demon seemed to be normal, if that was even possible for a demon. If we didn't know he was a full-fledged demon, I would have never guessed. Instead, he struck me as some overly inked biker. The part that bothered me the most was he could go invisible. Who knows how many times he'd watched us with Danica.

I was a bit jealous.

On top of the Reve situation, Danica was in a funk over what she was. I can't say I blamed her. I had wondered about it for months and so had Asher. The only one who seemed to push the idea of Lilith being her mother out of his head was Oliver. He'd much rather see the glass half full than half empty.

We landed in the middle of a loading dock outside an abandoned mall and stood in a line, looking at the dark building in front of us. I felt a chill sweep over me as a breeze gently blew.

I hoped Danica was all right without us with her. I had never been so scared in my life as she had stumbled out of my classroom, her nose gushing blood. When we got to her, she was already lying face down in a pool of red. When we had touched her, she felt like she was on fire.

Not how you want to see your girlfriend.

Oliver and I had taken her to the infirmary. We were told to go back to class to complete the final. I had refused to leave her side. Sue was already pissed that Michael had firmly told her that I was allowed to have a relationship with Danica. But me refusing to go back to my classroom to finish the final? That had tipped her over the edge.

I'd worry about my suspension later.

"What should we be looking for?" Oliver broke

the silence that had descended over our small group.

"Depends what we're up against," Reve answered from somewhere near Lucifer. Before we left, he decided to stay invisible as an element of surprise.

I still didn't completely trust him. He could have done something to Danica without us knowing. He could have been working for Lilith.

"Are we all clear on how to kill demons?" We all said yes in some shape or form. None of us had been specifically trained in killing demons. Apparently the risk of demons coming through the barrier to Earth was an impossibility.

Or so everyone thought.

Lucifer was scanning the area. For what, I wasn't sure. "This way. They came through over here." He was all business as he marched towards a chain link fence surrounding the building.

We followed like well-trained soldiers. We all carried swords we had grabbed from a weapons cache angels kept in the city. It hadn't been used in centuries.

To incapacitate a demon we needed to behead them or rip out their heart, then burn the body. The problem was that different demons had multiple heads or hearts in weird places. They might also be heavily shielded.

We squeezed through a hole cut in the chain link and made our way to a side door off a loading dock. The place was completely deserted and quiet, with graffiti covering the walls and trash thrown about.

The light was fading fast; it was nearly seven in the evening. We entered a large room that looked like a gutted section of the mall. The light coming in through skylights overhead cast eerie shadows across the floor. In the middle of the room were giant holes leading to the bottom floor of the mall. At some point, there had been a railing around them.

"Should we wait for the others?" I asked as we looked down into the darkness of the first level. Lucifer had called in reinforcements; they would be arriving soon.

Just as he started to answer, a low growl came from the darkness. My eyes searched in the direction of the sound and six beady red eyes looked back. The growl came again and this time a few more joined.

My heart rate quickened. I wasn't sure what was growling. I had a clue but didn't want to admit to myself what it was. I studied demons, but I certainly wasn't an expert.

"Is that a dog?" Oliver took a step closer to the edge. "Nope, definitely not a-"

The cement beneath his feet gave way and he dropped like a sack of potatoes. I saw a flash of white as he fell and then all hell literally broke loose.

Those six red eyes? It was a fucking hellhound,

except it was so unlike anything I'd studied that I was doubting if I had any business even being a Demonology teacher. It looked more like some kind of prehistoric dinosaur with spikes running along its three spines. Its three tails lit up with fire, sending light around the darkened recesses of the lower level. Then the thing split and formed three separate hounds.

Reading about demons is one thing, but seeing them in person is something else entirely. It felt like an out of body experience staring at a beast that had just split itself into three.

We all jumped down to the bottom level to find Oliver already fending off a humanoid-looking demon. It opened its mouth to reveal a circular ring of sharp teeth and a long tongue that lashed out to grab his wrist. It looked similar to a Demogorgon from *Stranger Things*.

He let out a scream and Asher swung his sword, cutting the tongue off, sending black blood across the floor. With one swift move, he took off its head. The loud, high-pitched screeching sound it made had me wanting to cover my ears.

"Stay close, these are some of the worst," Lucifer warned us. We were standing in a tight half-circle. "If one of them gets you alone... well, just don't let it get you alone. Stay in pairs. Don't let them surround us."

"We need to take care of this hellhound first. If it stays separated long enough each hound will form three bodies again and continue to split. It's a multiplier." Reve took his sword that Lucifer was holding for him. All I could see of him was the sword he was holding and his hand.

We made quick work of the hounds, taking their heads off. It was more difficult than I thought to remove a head. The movies made it seem so easy. We had no time to rest though because several other creatures zeroed in on us.

I glanced over at Lucifer, Olly, and Asher who were stabbing the ground. It looked like a million spiders were descending upon them. Lucifer's wings came out and he flew towards a woman that looked like a normal woman, except for her black eyes and the spiders pouring from her skin. She managed to jump at the last minute before his sword could connect with her. She disappeared into the darkness.

I managed to take down a demon that had the head of a man and body of a scorpion, but as the head flew, something from its tail hit my right arm, right in the middle of Charlie's face. At first, I just thought it was a splatter of dark demon blood it left behind, but then it started to burn and smoke. I wiped at it with my left hand, which was stupid, and I dropped to my knees as a burning sensation spread up my arms. It was eating away at my flesh.

Flashes of white from up above caught my eye as other angels arrived to help. The screeches from dying demons hit my ears, but I was struggling to move out of the way of the melee.

Arms took hold of me from behind and I was dragged backwards. It was Reve.

He stopped on the other side of an old set of escalators and sat me against the wall. The action was happening out of eyesight. If Reve was on the other team, I was a dead man.

"I have to cut it off." My eyes went wide at his words and I vehemently shook my head, words refusing to come out. "Just the flesh that has been touched. If I don't, it will spread and we'll have to cut off both your arms. If I don't do this you will die."

I looked at him pleadingly and then down at my arm where my tattoo was already destroyed by whatever the black substance was.

I shut my eyes and then nodded.

"I'm sorry I have to do this." He sounded pained at the thought of cutting into my flesh.

I could hear the shouts and sounds of demons on the other side of where he had dragged me. I kept my eyes shut and then he began to cut.

I WOKE as my body was jostled against a muscular chest. The smell of sulfur and ash was in the air and I opened my eyes to find Reve's face staring down at me.

I lifted my arm that had been cradled against my chest. Whatever it had looked like when he carved off the decaying flesh was now healed to a flawless new patch of skin. I could only see part of Margie's face. My children were gone.

The sense of loss was overwhelming and I clenched my eyes shut.

"Oliver was able to heal your arm. I'm sorry about your tattoo. I know how much they can mean." He spoke low, so only I could hear. I knew the others were near from the sounds of their feet shuffling on the floor as he made his way across the dark mall. "I'll fix it for you."

"How?" I managed to get the word out and a hiccup came after. I looked at my arm again. It might have been healed, but the whole thing looked like a layer of smooth scar tissue.

Angel tattoos were a complicated and painful process that involved several passes with a tattoo gun. When I had gotten mine back in the sixties the wait list for the one angel tattoo artist was several years long.

"I'll do it, if you'll let me." I grunted as he stopped and set me down. He took my elbow to steady me.

I glanced around at the twenty or so angels. Some looked worse for wear, but it seemed there were no casualties on our end. Asher and Oliver were walking several feet ahead of us with Lucifer in between them.

Lucifer reached into his pocket and pulled out his cell phone. He stopped abruptly and stood staring at his phone for several seconds before he took off running towards the exit.

Danica.

We took off after him, seeing him launch into the sky just as we came out of the door. As soon as we were far enough outside, Asher grabbed me and we shot into the sky too. He was a perceptive bastard, knowing I was still recovering from whatever that demon had hit me with.

We landed outside Asher's building and rushed into Danica's open door, nearly falling over each other in our haste. The first sight that greeted us was the doctor and assistant laying sprawled out on the floor. Oliver rushed to them.

Both of his hands lit up as he put one hand on the doctor and one on the assistant.

"Don't overdo it, angel baby," Asher said, stepping into the hallway leading to Danica's room.

I followed, with Reve behind me. Asher braced his hands on the doorframe, stopping us from rushing forward. Lucifer was on his knees by the side of the bed, his hands on the empty mattress.

"Lily... Lilith took her." Lucifer's voice shook. He gripped the sheets in his hand.

Asher stepped into the room so we could take in the scene. The room looked how we had left it, except instead of Danica on the bed, there was a crescent burned into the sheets.

Lucifer stood, clenching his fists next to his sides. Asher and I looked at each other and backed up towards the door. We felt the temperature jump at least ten degrees in the room.

"We'll find her." Reve was one brave mother-fucker for speaking. He even took a step farther into the room. Although, I guess if things really got heated, he could just ghost-out.

"This is my fucking fault." We ducked as a lamp was thrown across the room and shattered, sending shards of glass flying in our direction.

He moved so fast we barely had time to track his movements. First the lamp. Then the night-stand. Then the sheets on the bed.

Oliver shoved his way through us and tackled Lucifer onto the floor. I was starting to think what-ever demon poison had eaten my skin had somehow made it to my brain. I had to have just imagined Oliver taking Lucifer down and pinning him to the ground.

"Calm down!" He flipped him and twisted his arm behind him while putting his knee on his back. Was Oliver a police officer in a previous life? *Jesus.*

Lucifer struggled but then went limp under him, his shoulders shaking with sobs. Oliver let out a tired sounding sigh and we watched in awe, as we always did, as his hands glowed and spread to Lucifer.

"You know we can't locate her if we aren't

calm." Oliver's voice was shaking. He had healed too much.

He finally let Lucifer go and sat back on his ass against the side of the bed. He put his face in his hands and took deep breaths.

"She's not within a three-hundred-mile radius of here. That's as far as I can search. That, or she's being hidden."

Lucifer rolled over, staying on the floor, and stared up at the ceiling. He looked like shit, but I'm sure we all did. I certainly felt like it. A numbness had settled over me. I was sure I was going to wake up and this would be some nightmare Reve had somehow decided to torment us with.

I sat down in a chair that hadn't been destroyed and felt the weight of the day slam down on me. My job might as well be gone. My tattoo was gone. Danica was gone.

"She's not being hidden." Lucifer had his eyes shut, but his eyes were moving under his eyelids. "This was a message to me to come get her."

"What do you mean a message?" Asher lowered himself next to Oliver, their arms touching.

"She doesn't want Danica. She wants me." He stood then and walked over to the other side of the bed where his suit jacket was. He slid his arms into it, resolve in his movements. "They're in Shanghai."

"China?" Reve asked, sounding as confused as we all felt. "Why would she take her there? How did they get there so fast? Lilith can't fly, can she?"

"I don't know how. My guess is she has demon transport, but maybe she can fly. Are you coming with me or not?" He stopped in front of us and gave each of us a look. "She's going to need you four."

I stared up at him. At one point in time I had thought the angel was this untouchable, unbreakable king of the underworld. Now, staring up at him, he was much, much more than that. He was a worried father who loved his daughter and would do anything to get her back.

"We can rest once we get there. Regroup. Contact the others." He had quickly switched back to all business. "There are only three places we can land in the city."

We all got to our feet. I didn't even know if I could make it all the way to China with how exhausted I was. We walked outside to the small parking lot. It was the middle of the night and the street was quiet.

Lucifer took my hand and I raised an eyebrow at him.

"Don't want you to fall in the Pacific."

Our wings extended and we took off into the night sky.

Chapter Fifteen

Danica

*O*riginally, I thought we were going to be taking a private plane or helicopter to wherever it was Lilith was taking me.

Boy, was I wrong.

We didn't drive far from my apartment, but the area we were at was deserted. Waiting for us was a crazy-looking creature the size of a school bus.

"What is it?" Despite being scared shitless, I couldn't help but ask.

"What does it look like? I know you didn't do well in school, but you aren't stupid." The two men, who I assumed were her guards, laughed, and I deepened my frown.

"Maybe if I'd had a mother to help me, I would have done better in school."

She let out an exasperated sigh and turned

towards me. "You've always been destined for something greater than any human education could give you." She gestured towards the creature. "This is a fire dragon."

"Versus what? A water dragon?" I spat.

A dragon. A motherfucking dragon in a field. I felt like this was a setup for a joke you might find on a popsicle stick, or from some creeper at a bar.

"Exactly." The men laughed again and she started walking towards it. I kept my feet firmly planted on the ground.

"Can't we teleport there or something?" My brain was telling me to run but my body wasn't cooperating. I had a slight headache again too.

"Teleporting isn't a thing. If you're referring to how your father just seemingly appears and disappears, that is only him going through the barrier between Earth and Inferna. Now, let's go."

I already felt dizzy enough, I didn't need to ride on a... *oh my God*. I was looking at a dragon. Was it really a dragon? I squinted in its direction and confirmed. Yes, it was a dragon of some sort. It was solid black like tar and seemed to be bonier than the typical type. It was more of a snake with wings.

Was my mother the Mad Queen? She wasn't the Queen of England, that was for sure. I was hallucinating. My father was Lucifer and my mother was Lilith, but a dragon? The line had to be drawn somewhere and a motherfucking dragon was that line.

I took a step forward and stumbled, one of the bodyguards catching me. My vision was blurring again. That was the last thing I remembered.

I WOKE to the smell of something delicious. Thank fuck. It had all been one of my nightmares again. I'd seriously have to reconsider my concept of reality if I had actually ridden on a dragon.

I lengthened my body under the soft sheets and looked around the room. I sat straight up and took in the decor. It was modern and clean. Gray light was filtering in under the closed curtains.

It wasn't a nightmare, I was living it. I wasn't in *my* bed or any other bed I knew.

I stood and stretched, my body feeling refreshed. I felt completely fine with no signs of a fever or headache.

Someone, hopefully my mother and not one of the demon men, had changed me into a pair of black pajamas. Silk? I could never tell the difference between fabrics, but these pajamas felt like heaven against my skin.

I went to the window and pulled the curtains back. I was surprised to see trees outside the window, a window that had a key lock to prevent it from being opened. That was totally up to fire code.

I made my way to the bedroom door and put my ear against it to see if I could hear anything. I could hear sounds down the hall but nothing else. I tried the door and the handle turned.

Poking my head out, I took in the shiny dark wood running down the length of the hall where there were several closed doors. I walked down the hall towards the sounds and smells. Someone was cooking.

I entered a large living area and my eyes landed on my mother, who was sitting at a large dining room table, sipping coffee and staring at the screen of a laptop. Her eyes darted to me when I stepped into the room.

"Danica, please join me. John was just cooking us breakfast." She looked towards the kitchen and smiled.

I tentatively walked towards her and could finally see the man in the kitchen. John Senior looked older than the last time I had seen him, gray hairs peppering his dark hair. He turned his head towards me and gave me a smile.

"Where are we?" I stayed where I was. "And did we really ride a dragon here?"

She threw her head back and laughed. We even had the same laugh and I cringed. I wanted to be nothing like this woman. She had threatened the only family I had. They must be out of their minds with worry wondering where I was.

"It wasn't a dragon, but your reaction when I told you it was, was priceless. It was a hell serpent.

Please join me." She gestured to the chair to her right.

A hell serpent? As if that was any better than a dragon. Where was this so-called hell serpent now? I would have felt much better if it had been a dragon.

I moved towards the table but sat with one chair in between us, which only caused her to smile even more. I looked around the room. I could tell from the kitchen that wherever we were, we weren't in the United States anymore. Everything was more compact here and everything had a gloss to it. Not your typical American-style choices.

"We are in Shanghai. We have business here tomorrow night. John, bring her some coffee." She tapped her nails on the table. The more I watched her, the more similarities I was finding between us. I didn't like it.

"I don't drink coffee." A cup was set in front of me anyways, but I didn't touch it.

"You look much better this morning," John said as he stepped back after putting the coffee down. "I was afraid we'd made an error in our serum calculations."

"What serum?" I looked from him to Lilith. "Why is he even here?"

Lilith steepled her finger under her chin and then nodded her head back to the kitchen in a gesture to get John to leave.

"A serum with my blood. It was how we stopped the reaction you were having."

"Reaction?"

"It's been going on for quite some time, actually. Ever since you had such grievous injuries when we first took you. But with all the stress you've been under, the introduction of a demon into your sex life, and some poison, your angel blood couldn't keep the demon part of you locked away any longer."

"I don't understand." I scrunched my forehead in thought. I needed something to do with my hands so I picked up the coffee cup and drank down the bitter liquid. I cringed and shuddered at the taste.

"The roses. That really threw your angel blood off balance. Now the question is, just how much your demon blood was able to take hold. How do you feel? John will take a blood sample from you once we eat."

I gripped the edge of my chair to stop my hands from shaking and from throwing objects at her. I was so stupid coming here with her, but what choice did I have? I couldn't let everyone die because of my fear.

"I feel fine. What did you do to me? Blood doesn't work like that." I brought my hands to rest on the table and examined them, as if the skin would give me an answer.

John spoke from the kitchen. "*Human* blood

doesn't work like that, but you aren't human. Your blood was fifty percent angel and fifty percent demon. Since you are here on Earth, your angel blood is stronger. Giving you Lilith's blood should have decreased the angel blood significantly, especially with the stress you were under and the viruses I put on those thorns and roses."

I clenched my teeth to keep from whimpering.

"We've been running experiments on some of the blood we've collected from angels, and Lilith's blood destroys angel blood at a rate twice as fast as regular demon blood."

I felt sick and stood. "Excuse me. I need to use the restroom."

I took off down the hall and slammed the door shut behind me. I rushed into the bathroom and looked in the mirror. I looked just as I always had. I leaned forward on the counter and pulled my eyelids further apart to examine my eyes. Normal.

I let out a shaky breath and turned to lock the bathroom door. I needed a shower and a plan. My duffel bag was sitting on the bathmat and I picked it up. She had packed a bag for me. I shook my head in disbelief.

Lilith was a monster, but somewhere deep inside of her she at least had the heart to pack me a bag. I didn't know how to feel about that, because what could I feel? I hated her.

I stripped out of the pajamas that weren't mine and took my bra off, the note I had stuffed in it falling to the floor. I picked it up and unfolded the heart shaped note. It was cute and I cracked a smile despite the dire situation I was in.

DEAR DANICA,

I've never written a note to someone before. I'm sorry for acting like a "complete fucking asshole dick" last night (that's what Asher called me and I agree). I may have overreacted, but I was hurt that you would keep something like that from me. Now that I'm thinking about it, maybe I did deserve that. You don't owe me anything with how I once treated you.

I honestly don't care what you are. You are Danica Deville, my girlfriend, my love, my everything. As corny as that sounds, it's true. Even if you sprouted horns and a tail, I'd love you.

Please forgive me for acting like an idiot. I will make it up to you with orgasms. Asher tells me that orgasms are a great apology. So how many will it take?

Love and cookies,

Olly

I STARED down at the note written in flawless handwriting. It was simple, yet in that moment it was exactly what I needed to read. I refolded the note and buried it in my duffel bag. Hopefully it would make it back to California.

Would I ever get to go home?

I turned on the shower and stepped under the

hot water, my thoughts drifting to the angels I had left behind. Where were they right now? Had they survived the demons that made it through? Would they be able to find me?

I needed to make a plan to escape. Shanghai was a big city and it would be easy to slip away and hide among the throngs of people. But then what? I couldn't go to the police because I didn't even have my passport with me. What would I tell them? My evil, demon mother, *the* Lilith took me on a magical hell serpent ride?

That would get me a one-way ticket into China's finest mental institution.

Once showered and dressed, I walked down the hall and entered the living space where John was sitting, staring off into nothingness. I approached slowly and sat in a chair across from him.

"Why are you helping her?" The woman in question was nowhere to be seen and I needed to find out information.

The more I knew, the better I could plan an escape. The house we were in was like a fortress and I had yet to see the hell serpent or the two burly men anywhere. They were probably right outside, just waiting for me to attempt an escape.

"Why would I not help her?" He straightened in his seat and looked at me. "You're going to help her now, are you not?"

I chose my words carefully. "Not because I want to. What do you gain from helping her?"

He looked down the hall and then leaned forward on the couch, as if the few inches were going to give us privacy for what he was planning on saying.

"Freedom for my son." I stared back at him and raised my eyebrows, urging him to continue. "I am the closest in blood to the original Adam. It was a story that I thought was made up by my grandfather, so when I jokingly told my fraternity brothers about it, they dared me to try to summon Lilith. One of them had read a story about her being a demon that could be summoned."

"So you summoned her as a drunken frat boy, she showed up, and she forced you to be her little bitch?"

"Yes. I know it seems crazy, but it happened. Isn't all of it a bit crazy? I have pledged myself to her. Those were her terms. Pledge myself to her or she'd take my first born." He seemed defeated, like he'd rather be anywhere but here. "Whatever you do, don't pledge yourself to her."

Just as he finished speaking, Lilith's heels could be heard down the hall and his eyes widened. He sat back in his chair and returned to staring off into space.

"Danica. I'm glad to see you've rejoined us. We have business to discuss." She sauntered into the room, her eyes locked on John.

It was unclear if she had heard what he had

said, but if she had, well, I wasn't going to wish him the best.

"What business?" I kept my feet firmly planted on the ground, ready to run if I needed to. I wasn't sure where I'd run, but I'd find a way out if I needed to.

"You of course." She perched on the arm of the couch, right next to John, and jabbed her fingers into his hair before fisting it and pulling his head to the side. "Go check on our guests."

She shoved his head away and John stood; he looked like he was about to cry. I watched as he retreated from the room and wondered who she was referring to as guests.

"Now. It's time to talk about your future at my side." She turned her body towards me and I shifted in my seat, trying to make the distance between us wider.

"I don't want to be at your side." She frowned at my response. "I want nothing to do with you."

"I have big plans for Earth. Inferna is getting a little stuffy and my demons are getting restless." She stood and started to pace behind the couch. "You'll want to be by my side when I get them through the barrier."

"Why? Why are you doing this?" I watched her back and forth movements. I wanted to stand and pace too, but stayed glued to the seat. I wouldn't let her see just how similar we were. She'd use it against me.

"It's all part of a bigger plan, years and years in the making. Now all the stars have aligned and I'll be able to take back what is mine." She stopped pacing and looked at me. "What's yours."

"And what's that?" I had an uneasy feeling in my belly. She really was batshit crazy.

"Everything."

I let out an uncomfortable laugh and then smacked my hand over my mouth. I hadn't meant to laugh, but I was starting to think this was some kind of elaborate prank. Maybe this woman was a former Divine 7 and it was all a setup.

"How many people do you think live in Shanghai?"

I frowned and lowered my hand from my mouth. I shrugged because I honestly had no clue.

"Twenty-four million." She smiled and resumed her trot behind the couch. I was glad there was a barrier between us. "Now, imagine a hell serpent being let loose." She paused. "Are you imagining it?"

"You wouldn't." I knew she was evil, but she wasn't *that* evil, was she?

"My demons do as I ask." She snapped her fingers. "I could level this city with a simple command. You could too, with the right training."

My eyes widened and I felt all the blood drain from my face. I swallowed the lump in my throat.

"Those angels and humans can offer you nothing. How do you think four men seemingly fell in love with you at first sight?" I wanted her to stop talking, so I covered my ears with my hands. She just spoke louder. "Once they find out that you can control them, manipulate their minds, they'll run for the hills."

"No. I never manipulated them!" I let my hands fall to my lap.

"Oh, but you did. You just didn't realize it. Do you really think they would love you otherwise? You are nothing more than a silly girl. Even your father can't stand to be around you. Why do you think he was never around when you were growing up?"

I took in her words and looked down at my hands. Part of me didn't believe a word she said, but the other part of me knew it made sense.

"Don't hurt them. Anyone, please." A calmness spread over my body. I didn't want to play into her plans, but I also couldn't let her kill millions of people.

"Very well. Tomorrow night we will be attending a gala where a very precious artifact will be on display. You are going to steal it for me."

"What artifact? Why can't you steal it yourself?" I spoke cautiously.

"I can't touch it, but I'm pretty sure since you can get onto academy grounds that you can." She laughed and sat down on the couch, crossing her legs. "You're going to steal the Holy Grail."

Holy shit.

Chapter Sixteen

Oliver

J felt the change in the air a few miles from the boarder of China. The air was thick and muggy, like an old house that had been closed up for too long. I was exhausted, but Asher had hold of me the entire flight, although it was all of a few minutes.

There were a few places in the city we could land. Shanghai had strict flying rules due to the population density and the vast amount of street cameras. The camera system was so good, it was rumored that if someone stole something, the cameras would track them all the way to where they lived.

We landed on top of the Peninsula Hotel. No one could see us when we were flying, but if you were on the street and suddenly someone seemed to magically appear in front of you, you'd start asking questions. Or freak out. In large cities, landing was tricky.

We took the elevator down to the ground floor and Lucifer worked his magic at the front desk. They seemed to immediately know who he was, greeting him as Mr. Deville.

"How many rooms do I need to get?" He turned his head towards Asher and me. We were standing next to each other. Why did everyone keep looking at us like that? It wasn't like we had announced to the world that we had shared a kiss or two.

"We can share two rooms. I don't mind sharing with Reve, as long as he doesn't snore." Tobias surprised the heck out of me sometimes. One minute he hated Reve, the next he seemed to be buddies with him.

"I can afford separate rooms, son. Don't feel you need to share just because I'm footing the bill." Lucifer's voice lacked its normal vibrato. He was letting his guard down around us.

Tobias's face softened. "It's fine. We probably should bond or whatever it is we're supposed to do when we share a..." He didn't finish his sentence.

"I'm fine sharing a room. I don't sleep anyways." Reve had his arms cross over his chest and was tapping his foot on the marble floor. His eyes were dark and he didn't make eye contact with any of us. "I need to go hunt."

Hunt? What the hell was he talking about? I looked at Asher and he shrugged.

Lucifer nodded and turned back to the counter to book three rooms. He hadn't even waited for a response from me or Asher.

"What do you mean by hunt? Like a vampire?" I couldn't help but ask, my curiosity probably my most well-developed trait. Although it was also the trait that got me in the most trouble.

"I feed off the fear in nightmares I create or enter into. I haven't had to feed in a while because of Danica." He stopped and frowned. "I should go."

He walked away and turned down a hall. I didn't think I wanted to find out what happened when a demon was starving.

Lucifer handed us our keycards. We were given river-view rooms, which brightened my mood just a tad. I had seen pictures of Pudong, which was the part of Shanghai across the river with all of the tall skyscrapers, and was curious to see how glorious it was in person.

The hotel staff was going to send clothing to our rooms. We hadn't bothered packing anything. We must have been a sight with disheveled clothing, messy hair, and faces pinched tight with worry. We looked like bedraggled travelers who had been mugged. If they only knew what we had been up to.

"Let's get some rest. I'll make some calls. There's not much we can do right now. I know she's here.

There are too many angels packed together and I'm too tired to directly pinpoint her." He walked towards the elevators and we followed.

He scratched at his arm while we waited for the elevator and pulled back the sleeve of his shirt. One of those damn spiders from the mall must have bit him. I reached forward and healed it.

"Thanks, Oliver. I didn't even know it was there." I shuddered, remembering the large spiders that had crawled out of the demon's skin. It was the creepiest thing I had ever seen. Luckily, one of the other angels had caught her, ripped out her heart, and burned her body.

It was gruesome, images that would haunt me for a while, but killing a demon was no easy feat. I just hoped we got them all and the clean-up crew had disposed of them before humans found the evidence of our battle.

We rode the elevator up to our floor in silence and went our separate ways. Asher opened the door to the room we would share and I walked down the hallway entrance, past the closet and bathroom, to the main room. It had floor to ceiling windows and a view of across the river.

There was one bed.

I had never seen anything quite like the skyline. Los Angeles was a big city but had nothing on this.

I felt Asher move across the room towards me, my neck prickling with his approach. He was so unpredictable. So volatile. I didn't quite know what to do half the time. Which is why I always touched him, hoping to curb whatever storm he had brewing.

The thing was, I also touched him when I knew he was fine. Touching always seemed to put him in a better head space. It took the edge off, but lately it only amped up the intensity between us.

He pretended it didn't affect him, but I could see it in his eyes. I could feel it in the way he'd touch my arm. In the way he'd put a hand on my lower back for a mere second when he passed by.

And then there was that kiss.

We had been avoiding being alone with each other since the hot kiss we shared. Well, *he* had. I wanted nothing more than to be close to him. To explore what Danica had set in motion.

I shuddered at the thought that I had once mistreated her. She was more divine in spirit than any of the angels. She had brought us together and been nothing but accepting of whatever was to be.

"Are you doing all right?" I asked as he stopped next to me.

"It comes and goes. I'm glad you're here." He stared out the window and put his hand against it. "Where do you think she is?"

"She could be anywhere. I mean, look at this place. It's like finding a needle in a haystack. If anyone is going to be able to find her though, it's Lucifer." I tried to sound sure. I could locate people I knew well with ease, but when angels were in mass, it was difficult, at least for me being so new.

"What are you seeing?"

"It's just a sea of white light. There are too many angels in such close proximity." I sighed and leaned my forehead against the window. "I can't even do that right."

"What are you talking about? Lucifer is even struggling to locate her now that we're here."

"Everything I touch seems to get messed up. The Holy Grail, Levi, Dani, you."

"I hardly think you had anything to do with Levi being fucked up. He was fucked up to begin with. As for Dani, how is her being taken by her own mother your fault?"

"I was so angry with her for not telling us about what was going on. I'm supposed to protect her. What if..." I banged my head lightly on the window. My brain hurt. I was second guessing every decision I'd ever made.

"What if what?" Asher prompted, turning and propping his shoulder against the window.

I was distracted by his nearness. Whenever he was near me, I couldn't resist the urge to reach out and touch him. The last thing I needed to be thinking about at the moment was all the ways I wanted to touch him. We were having a serious discussion. We'd never talked like *this* before.

"What if the whole reason I was created was for this moment? I was never given a purpose in heaven and all angels are given a purpose. But here I am, Oliver Morgan. First archangel since the originals, and I was just left to roam the Great City in heaven? Doesn't sound quite right. No direction. No reason. No purpose. Then one day I just felt this pull towards the religious artifacts and the cup caught my eye. The need to come to Earth and try it out was so strong I couldn't resist. What if that happened for a reason? So I'd be at the academy. So I'd meet Danica. So I'd meet Tobias." I took a breath. "So I'd meet you."

"I guess that's plausible." Asher brought his hand to his jaw and rubbed his stubble. I tracked the movement, my forehead turned slightly so I could watch him.

"My existence didn't make sense. Nothing around me made sense. Until Danica and now you. You make sense to me."

Asher's face softened and his hands dropped to his sides. It was a look I was only used to seeing when he looked at Danica. His stormy eyes looked back into mine, searching for something.

"You sure do know how to sweet talk someone, don't you?" His voice was gentle. "I don't know what to do with these thoughts and feelings I have towards you. With Danica, it's so natural, but with you..."

My heart sank and I turned my eyes back to the Oriental Pearl Tower across the Huangpu River.

He was quiet for a few moments before

speaking again. "With you, it's so new. Definitely unexpected and unfamiliar territory. Being intimate with a man is not something I know how to do. Hell, it's new to you too. It's like I'm an innocent virgin all over again." He paused. "Would you even want to explore that side of things?"

I could feel his eyes on me as my face and ears felt like they were on fire. If he only knew how I'd fantasized about him and the things he would do to me and the things I would do to him. The thoughts I'd had of him were sinful enough to make me wonder if a trip to hell was in my future.

"Have you thought about it? Being with me?" I bit my lip and watched as a barge that had tires around the entire edge made its way slowly down the river. A yacht was not far behind.

"I have. I've thought a little too much about it. What it would be like to have a man's mouth, your mouth, on mine, wrapped around me, your hands on me." His voice was raspy.

My cock twitched at his words and I shut my eyes. "Have you thought about what you'd do to me?"

I felt him move closer and he trailed a finger down my arm and grabbed my hand. He held it in his and started drawing shapes in the palm, just like I always did with him. I couldn't keep back the small noise that escaped my mouth.

He spoke almost in a whisper, despite us being the only ones in the room. Not quite next to my ear, but close enough that when he let out a breath, I could feel it.

"There's so much I want to do to you, angel baby. I'd start by kissing the fuck out of you like that first time. I'd lay you on the bed and grind my dick against yours. I imagine that would feel amazing. Don't you think so?"

I grunted and let out a breath of air as he put his lips against my palm and swirled his tongue in the center.

"Then I'd take your hand and put it right here." He moved my hand down to his erection and pressed my hand onto it. "So you'd know just how turned on the thought of being with you makes me."

He moved his hips against our joined hands and groaned in the back of his throat. "Fuck, Oliver. I've never wanted a man before."

I moved my hand away from him and turned so I was facing him. I was slightly taller than him and his eyes landed directly on my mouth. I licked my bottom lip and that was all the invitation he needed to cup both of my cheeks and take my lips in a blistering kiss.

This was more urgent than our first, needier. We both needed each other in this moment. Needed the comfort. Needed the passion. Needed the distraction.

"Asher." His lips left mine and his teeth scraped down my jawline.

There was nothing soft or gentle about his mouth and teeth as they grazed across my skin. He was greedy and took me with his lips and teeth. He trailed his tongue along my Adam's apple and I put my hand against the window to steady myself.

"Are we going to do this? For real?" he mumbled against my neck. "Because I think I'm about to reach the point of no turning back. So if you don't want this, you need to tell me." He kissed under my ear and bit down on my earlobe, causing me to gasp. "Because if you don't stop me, I'm about to fucking take you, Oliver Morgan."

I moaned and grabbed a fist full of his hair and pulled his lips back to mine. He took my bottom lip in his teeth and then sucked it into his mouth. I had always imagined this happening so gently, but screw that. This was what I needed. What I wanted.

We stumbled towards the bed in the center of the room and fell onto the mattress on our sides, our lips never breaking contact. In a way it felt wrong to be doing this with Asher while Danica was out there somewhere.

"Maybe this isn't the right time to be doing this," I managed to get out as we broke for air. "With everything that's going on."

Asher looked back at me and his eyes dropped to my mouth where he took a finger and pressed it into my bottom lip.

"When is the right time?" His finger trailed down the front of my shirt and then hooked into the front of my jeans. I almost forgot about what I had asked.

Words were failing me as he popped the button and slid down the zipper. My breath came in heavy inhales and exhales. I was surprised I even remembered to breathe. I had wanted this for so long. Not just with Asher. I had wanted to explore this side of my sexuality.

"That's quite the answer." He was amused at my lack of words.

His hand dipped inside my pants and his fingers gripped me through my boxer briefs. I couldn't help but thrust my hips.

What was I so worried about?

He pushed at my shoulder so I'd roll onto my back and hovered over me, his lips close to mine, but not touching.

"You know, when I first met you, I didn't like you." His hand slid into my boxers and pulled my cock out. I shut my eyes as he gripped it in his hand. "But then, I don't know. You just started fucking caring about me too much."

"Do you care about me?" The question had crossed my mind several times. He didn't exactly give off warm and fuzzy vibes. Plus, before Danica, he was a notorious womanizer. He said so himself one night on the couch. I would hope I wasn't just going to be another notch on his belt.

"Yes." He ran his thumb up the underside of

my cock and swiped his finger over the head. "If I didn't, I wouldn't be willing to try this."

I had no coherent words left, so I gripped the back of his head and pulled his lips back to mine. He parted his lips and I moved my tongue inside, tangling with his. His hips moved and he thrust his dick against my leg as he slid his hand up and down my shaft.

He pulled away and sat back on his heels, staring down at me, my erect dick pointing straight at him. His eyes moved downward and took me in.

"Danica always complains that blowjobs make her jaw hurt. I wonder if it's true. What do you think?" He moved his hands up and down my thighs a few times before his hands gripped my pants and boxers and pulled them down.

"Maybe it's like a muscle and you just have to use it enough," I said, somehow managing to get words to come out of my mouth in a complete, coherent thought.

Asher threw his head back and laughed. Things had been so tense lately, it was a pleasant sight to see. "Please say that to Dani and make sure I'm around when you do."

"I can't say anything to her until we've run some experiments." I looked at his lips. "And since you've received the most blowjobs out of the two of us, it's only scientifically appropriate for your mouth to be the first test subject."

"Is that so?" Asher ran his finger over the bead of pre-cum at my slit.

He was slowly killing me with his torture. I had noticed he had two extreme versions in the bedroom. Hard and fast, or slow and teasing. There was no in between with him.

"Are you going to suck my dick or not?" The words left my mouth before I could stop them. He had wound me up tight like a rubber band stretched between two fingers. I was about ready to snap and make a mess and he had barely even touched me.

He smirked down at me. "I was thinking that maybe we should shower. I need to relax a little and you seem to have forgotten that you had a tongue that wasn't mine wrapped around your arm earlier."

I groaned and pushed myself up on my fore-arms. "You're a tease."

He stood up and offered me his hand, which I begrudgingly took. I followed him to the bathroom, shedding my clothes as I went, since I already had my pants down anyways.

Asher turned on the shower and then looked at me in the mirror. He might have been taking charge a minute ago, but now he looked nervous. I had no misgivings about us, whatever it was that we were now.

He turned towards me as I stepped closer. He shut his eyes as I unbuttoned his pants. I was so used to him taking charge of situations, that this new dynamic felt strange. A good strange; definitely a strange that made my dick even harder.

He pulled off his shirt as I pushed his pants down his well-defined legs. I always thought I'd be turned on by abdominal muscles or even strong shoulders on a man, but Asher's legs were perfect.

We climbed into the shower that had two showerheads. I moaned as the warm water hit my body. I guess I did need a shower. We didn't speak as we washed ourselves.

I finished before Asher and leaned back against the shower wall, the steam enclosed in the shower, making it feel like a sauna.

I shut my eyes and brought my hand down to my dick. Asher made a noise and I opened my eyes as he stepped forward and pressed against me, our dicks touching.

"What are you doing to me?" He reached over and squirted body wash in his hand. He buried his face in my neck and took the both of us in his slick hand. "Fuck."

His grip was strong, and as he slid his hand up and down our joined cocks, I felt my balls tingle. I wasn't going to last long with his hands *and* dick on me.

My hands slid down his chest and I put my hand over his on our dicks. We moaned into each other as his hand tightened and our hips thrust together. I bit his bottom lip and then sucked it into my mouth.

He pushed closer to me and his other hand reached around me and gripped my ass, his nails digging into the sensitive flesh. My body shook and my knees felt unsteady as my orgasm crashed into me, spilling onto us. Asher let out a curse as he came.

We stood panting against the shower wall, coming down from the high of our releases.

"I'm exhausted." The sound of the water hitting the tiles was lulling me to sleep.

We cleaned off and then climbed into bed. The sun was barely rising as our heads hit the pillows and we drifted off to sleep in each other's arms.

Chapter Seventeen

Danica

I stood in front of the mirror and stared back at a woman I didn't recognize. My hair was pulled into a chignon and my makeup was simple with a bright red lip. My dress was a floor length, black lace gown with cap sleeves and a plunging neckline.

I guess if I was going to have to steal the Holy Grail, I was going to do it in style.

I shouldn't be going through with it, but how could I not? I didn't want to be at fault for millions of people dying. I knew that, regardless of my choice, she would steal the artifact anyways. Might as well save some people while I was at it.

What she even wanted with the Holy Grail was beyond me.

Maybe she had a wine drinking problem.

I had decided to detach myself from the situation. I was a robot, going through the motions. I could run, but she'd find me. Or she'd just kill everyone. She was a psychopath.

I dug in the duffle bag and found the letter from Olly. I had a feeling I wouldn't be coming back after this, so I shoved it in my bra.

I slid on the heels left by the door and walked out of the bedroom. My palms were sweaty and I wiped them down my lace covered thighs. It really was a gorgeous gown. Too bad it was tainted by the one who had given it to me.

I walked into the living room to find Lilith dressed in a burgundy velvet trumpet-style gown. The sleeves were long and the deep V neckline accentuated the necklace she wore. I took several steps closer to her and realized it was the lily necklace that had been in my jewelry box.

"You stole it," I said flatly, stopping several feet from her.

She brought her hand to the pendant and brought it away from her skin to look down at it. "You're insinuating that it wasn't mine to begin with."

I rolled my eyes. "Where's John?" I had assumed he'd be joining us.

"He has more pressing things to deal with." She sauntered over to me and looped her arm through mine. I tried to pull away but her grip on my arm was strong. "Are you clear on the plan?

My sources tell me that we will be in good company tonight. I don't want you to get any grand ideas in that head of yours. My hell serpent is ready to go if you do."

I nodded, not trusting myself to speak. If I did, I would give her a piece of my mind and what I had to say wasn't nice.

We exited into the garage where a black SUV was waiting with the two goons from before. They were dressed in tuxedos, and had they not manhandled and laughed at me back in California, I would have said they were handsome.

One climbed into the driver's seat, with Lilith taking the passenger side. I climbed into the back. The door locks engaged and we backed out of the garage.

"Those are childproof, so don't get any ideas," the goon with me in the back said. His voice was smooth as silk and I wondered what kind of demon he was.

I stayed silent as we pulled out of the housing development and onto a highway. We crossed over a river that had a bridge that looked like it had giant wishbones holding it up. I just stared out the window, in awe at the massive city that was outside.

After about thirty minutes, we pulled up to a hotel and waited in a long line of taxis and vehicles to be let out at the entrance.

"What kind of event is this?" I asked, finally breaking the silence.

"It's a gala auction," Lilith said as her door was opened and she got out of the SUV.

"No funny business in there, you got that? Hell serpents are hungry as fuck. Remember that," the goon next to me warned. He got out and I followed.

We entered into a ballroom that was already packed with people dressed to the nines in tuxedos and gowns. We blended in perfectly, except for the stolen glances towards Lilith.

As much as I didn't want to admit it, she was striking and had a commanding presence about her. There was a large dance floor set up in the front of the ballroom with a stage on the other side of it. Couples floated across the floor, looking as if they were part of a royal court.

It reminded me of Reve.

Where were my guardians right now? They had so quickly become engrained in my life and being away from them made me anxious.

We sat down at a table near the edge of the dance floor and a glass of wine was shoved in front of my face by Lilith.

"You're fidgeting. Follow the plan and every-thing will be fine." When I didn't take the wine glass from her, she set it down on the table. "Think of it this way. You are righting a wrong that happened long ago."

I made a noise in my throat. "And what wrong is that? Didn't you get pissed off that you couldn't be on top? Seems kind of childish to throw this big a tantrum."

The smile she had fell and she narrowed her eyes. "The internet is the worst invention known to man. Do you believe everything you read?" I shook my head. "I was created from nothing and promised everything. I stood up for myself as a woman and what did that get me?"

"Bitterness?"

She laughed and stood. She looked across the dance floor and a smile lit up her face. "Right on time. Your father always did have perfect timing."

I followed her gaze and saw my father standing alone on the other edge of the dance floor. He was staring right at Lilith, his gaze unwavering. His eyes then landed on me before quickly rising back to follow Lilith, who was moving around the perimeter of the floor towards him.

"I don't know if I believe that this goblet they have is the Holy Grail." I turned my head towards the voice, surprised to hear English. My eyes widened at the table full of businessmen at the next table over. A few of them were well known in the United States.

"Supposedly, a deep-sea fishing boat caught it in their cage. They said it was buoyant, which is odd, wouldn't you say?"

"Only a fool would spend their money on something like that."

I lost track of Lilith and my dad. I stood,

searching for them and found them on the dance floor. Together.

My heart jumped into my throat taking in the sight. Lucifer looked tense. I stepped forward to the edge, keeping my eyes on them. They moved in sync with each other as they glided across the floor.

Why was he not coming to rescue me? Maybe he knew what was at stake.

"Danica." I nearly jumped out of my skin as Olly appeared beside me. Damn him and his sneaky ways. "We have to go while she's distracted."

"I can't." I spoke low enough that the goons a few feet away couldn't hear. "She's going to kill a lot of people if I don't do what she asks."

He took my hand and I relaxed the tiniest amount. I wanted to run away with him, but too much was on the line.

"And what about you?" he whispered. I could feel his hand shaking in mine.

"She won't kill me. She wants me to rule with her." Hearing it come from my lips made me cringe.

"Rule what? You can't seriously be considering-" Just then, the fire alarm went off.

The two goons grabbed Olly and yanked him away from me. I gave him a look that I hope conveyed how sorry I was, then dashed across the dance floor through the throngs of people moving towards the exits.

I made my way around to the back of the stage

and walked right up to the two security guards who were making no move to leave.

I took a deep breath and balled my fists at my sides. Lilith had given me my first lessons on being her daughter. With the right motivation, I could control anyone or anything with darkness in them. John and the security guards hadn't enjoyed my training.

"I'm going to need for you to leave." I had the motivation and they had the darkness.

At first they seemed confused, and I wondered if they knew English, but then they walked past me, leaving me alone.

The auction items were behind the stage curtain, displayed in cases that could be rolled out when needed. I climbed up and stood in front of the Holy Grail. It's gold and silver design gleamed unnaturally and I felt a strong pull towards it.

It wanted me to take it.

I lifted the cover and grabbed it, the cool metal sending goosebumps up my arms. It felt powerful in my hands and I quickly made my way towards the side exit. Lilith was going to meet me just outside.

As soon as I was through the fire exit door, I knew something was wrong. Screams erupted from around the corner and I rushed down the sidewalk to peek around the edge of the building.

At the front of the hotel were swarms of evacuated people, and right in the middle was a large brawl that had my heart stopping. Right in the middle of it were the goons, Lucifer, Tobias, Asher, and Olly.

I took a step around the corner when a hand clamped on my arm and pulled me back, the nails of the owner digging into my arm. Lilith snatched the cup away from me and wrapped it in a cloth napkin.

"Let's go." She was pulling me across the crosswalk. Sirens could be heard in the distance, but were still far away.

"I got you what you wanted. Let me go!" I knew the plan wasn't for her to set me free, but it was worth a shot. When we were on the sidewalk, I planted my feet firmly.

"Let her go, Lilith." Reve's voice came from the side and Lilith stopped in her tracks, her head tilting to the side and the grin I was becoming all too familiar with spreading across her face.

"Show yourself, *Reve*." I did not like the tone her voice had. It was guttural and threatening.

Reve appeared, dressed in a tuxedo. He took a step forward and I begged him with my eyes to turn and run away.

"You have some balls coming here tonight. Does Danica know about us? About how you once pledged yourself to me?" She sounded amused.

My eyes widened and I watched Reve back up a step. "That's in my past. I'm no longer your slave."

"I beg to differ. Come here." I watched in horror as Reve obeyed her command and stopped in front of us. "How long has it been since you gave someone a vision?"

Reve paled. A small drop of blood escaped his mouth. He was biting himself to keep from answering.

"Answer me." I heard a noise behind me and a knife appeared in front of me. "Or I'll ruin her pretty little face."

I nearly went cross-eyed looking down at the knife now pressed against my chest. This was not part of the plan she had laid out for us. She wouldn't really cut my face, would she?

Who was I kidding? She would if it meant she got what she wanted.

"I haven't. Not for centuries." As he spoke, I could see the blood on his teeth. My knees trembled at the sight.

"I think tonight is a good night to rekindle that part of you. We'll start with all the people at the front of the hotel. You're to give them a vision of their worst nightmare come to life."

"There are hundreds! It will kill me!" His body was shaking and he backed up a step towards the hotel. He seemed to be fighting the compulsion. "Don't do this, Lilith."

"It's already done." The knife pressed a little harder against my chest. "And Reve? I am not Lilith to you."

"Your highness." His words came out stuttered

as he bowed to her. Then he turned and walked towards the front of the hotel.

"What have you done?" I whispered. She lowered the knife and pulled me down the sidewalk towards a waiting black SUV.

She didn't answer me. We were feet away from the vehicle when my dad landed in front of it, blocking the doors.

"Lilith." His wings retracted and he took a step forward.

Lilith's arm tightened around me and she backed up several steps, dragging me along with her. I stumbled in my shoes but managed to stay upright.

She brought her other arm back and threw the goblet towards the SUV. My eyes followed it as it landed in John's hands. He slid into the passenger seat as three men got out of the back. They were different from the two that had been with us earlier.

"Lilith, give me my daughter." His voice held no emotion, but his eyes told a different story. He was pissed and scared.

She held the sharp blade to my throat, the edge digging into my skin. I could feel the blood trickle down my neck.

My dad held his hands up and stayed where he was. His eyes were troubled, and his mouth drawn in a tight line.

Lilith laughed behind me, the movement

causing the knife to dig into my skin. All it would take was one good swipe and I'd be a goner.

"I can't be beat, Lucifer. Danica really was the best thing I could have done for myself. I was able to give myself at least another thousand years. To think all it takes to have immortality is a cup and some of your own offspring's blood. I have no use for her now."

My eyes teared up. A few tears escaped the corners and slid down my cheeks.

"If she's of no use to you now, why not let her go? What do you want? Just don't hurt her." He took a step towards us and she backed up, closer to the railing separating us from the river.

"Dad." I pleaded with my eyes. He had a determined look on his face.

His eyes met mine and his lip trembled as Lilith answered him.

"You know what I want. You've known since I had her the first time."

He let out a shaky breath and a tear slid down his cheek. He nodded and I knew she had wanted more than just the Holy Grail tonight.

"Don't, please!" I wanted to run to him and beg him not to play into her plan, whatever it was. The three men flanked him, two to the sides and one behind him.

"I love you, Danica. Whatever happens, know that."

The men grabbed him and one stabbed a

needle into his neck, plunging a black substance into his vein. His eyes went glossy and his knees gave out.

"You fool." Lilith laughed and then plunged the knife into my chest.

His eyes went wide and his mouth opened in a silent scream as I reached my shaking hands to the knife. I looked at it in disbelief and then back at my father.

I stumbled backwards as I watched them drag my dad by his arms to a waiting van and throw him in the back.

"He's always thought too much with his heart. Not so much with his brain." Lilith stood in front of me, her eyes devoid of any human emotion. "I had hoped for you to be by my side, but now that you have bonded with all four of those guardians of yours, I can't risk you getting in the way of my plans."

"I'm just a girl. I..." The pain in my chest prevented me from saying more.

"You aren't just a girl. I think you know that." With those words, she placed her hands on my cheeks. "My beautiful daughter. If only..."

If only what? But I never got my answer, because her hands lowered to my shoulders and shoved me over the railing and into the river.

Chapter Eighteen

Water filled my lungs as the initial impact of the water sent me under. I struggled to move towards the surface. The knife was still lodged in my chest and I was too afraid to pull it out. My head finally surfaced and I coughed violently, the taste of copper and dirt in my mouth.

The shore seemed so far away and my vision blurred. My ears didn't seem to be working, no sound reaching them. They felt numb. I felt numb.

I didn't want to die in a river.

I felt myself sinking again. My head had just gone back under when arms wrapped around me and I shot into the sky. We landed on the sidewalk and I was laid on the cement.

Asher stared down at me, his hair dripping water onto my face.

"Fuck, fuck, fuck!" I couldn't hear him

completely, but that certainly sounded like what he was saying.

I opened my mouth to speak and coughed. I realized how difficult it was to breathe as I tried to inhale and felt like I was getting no air. My hands went to the knife and Asher grabbed my wrists, stopping me.

I was starting to panic, air not getting inside like I needed it to.

Olly appeared next to Asher and his hands went to my chest. He shook his head and Asher yelled something at him. My eyes fluttered shut.

~

"DANICA."

My eyes popped open at the sound. I was in a large room with a single bed in the middle of it. Everything was white. Chinese hospitals were strange. Sterile.

My hands went to my chest, but the only thing I found was the white fabric of a top. I sat up and scanned the room. I definitely wasn't in Kansas anymore.

"Hello?" My voice echoed in the room and made me shudder. *Shit*. Was I dead?

This wouldn't be the first time I thought I was dead, but I also hadn't been in a white room with nothing but myself and a bed.

"You have to wake up. Your job is not done yet." The voice came from nowhere and sounded an awful lot like Morgan Freeman.

"You have got to be kidding me. Reve, if this is you playing a prank, I'm going to cut you." I swung my legs over the side of the bed and eyed the door on the other side. It gleamed like it was made from a thousand diamonds.

"This is not a prank, child. You just had surgery. Your blood can't heal you from your injuries."

"Why do you sound like Morgan Freeman? That's a little cliché, don't you think?"

The voice chuckled. "Or is he the cliché?"

I stood and walked towards the door. "Why can't I heal? Am I a demon now?"

He laughed again, the deep baritone sound making me want to smile. I reached for the handle of the door but it wouldn't turn.

"The angel part of your blood has always been stronger and has fought off the demon blood from taking over. Lilith attempted to disrupt that balance. She was unsuccessful."

"So what am I?" I looked at the ceiling as if it held all the answers. It seemed to be speaking, so maybe it actually did.

"When it's your time, the door will open for you."

"That doesn't answer my question." I rolled my eyes at the ceiling and the voice laughed again.

"You are your father's daughter."

Dad. Where was he? I opened my mouth to ask but the room started to spin.

A DISTANT PHONE ringing woke me. My eyes adjusted to the dim light. Asher and Olly were on a bench seat by the window, Olly with his head in Asher's lap. Tobias was in a chair next to the bed, his cheek resting on his hand.

My tongue darted to my dry lips and I raised a hand to them. I stared at the heart rate monitor clamped onto my finger and then at the IV taped to the top of my hand.

"You had surgery," Reve's quiet voice said from right next to the bed.

I startled and my hand went to my chest where I could feel thick bandages through the rough material of the hospital gown. I turned my head in the direction of his voice.

I had thought he had gone off to die.

"Tobias saved me. He claims he owed me for saving him." He was whispering and his voice came closer. "The short time I projected visions weakened me quite a bit though. I won't be able to get out of this form until I go feed. I wanted to wait until you woke up."

"Reve." My word came out more as air. I cleared my throat and tried again. "Reve."

My brain felt a bit foggy and I didn't understand what he meant by feed. I shifted in the bed and winced and sucked in air as pain radiated from my chest down to the tips of my fingers.

Tobias stirred in the chair and his eyes slowly cracked open. He blinked several times and then sat up straight and leaned forward, taking my hand.

"You're awake." I just nodded in reply and looked back to the other side of the bed where Reve was. Or at least where I thought he was.

"I'll be back," Reve said. "I love you, Danica."

I felt the stirring of air near my face and knew it was him. *I love you too.*

Tobias stood and walked around the end of the bed to a rolling tray that had a pitcher and cup. He poured water in the cup and put a straw in it.

He pushed a button on a controller and my bed moved so I was sitting up a little. It hurt, but I was desperate for water. After a few sips, I let out a sigh and cleared my throat again.

"My dad."

Tobias put the cup back and sat back down heavily. He looked over at Asher and Olly, still sleeping and oblivious.

"I should wake them up." He stood again and shook Asher's shoulder.

Asher jerked awake, jostling Olly's head, almost causing him to fall off the window seat they were on.

"My dad," I repeated. His face was the last thing I remembered.

Tobias sat back down and took my hand again. Asher and Olly both stood behind him.

"Where is he?" I felt a tear slip down my cheek. It was a feeling I was becoming well acquainted with.

"Dani." Olly sat on the edge of my bed and took my other hand. "We don't know where he is. The other archangels have been looking for him, but he vanished."

"Is he dead?" I felt my chest tightening as the words left my lips.

"Reve thinks she took him to Inferna." Asher stayed behind Tobias and looked at all the wires and tubes hooked up to me.

I wanted him to come to me, to touch me, but didn't know if I trusted myself to make any requests. What if everything they felt and did was because I had somehow manipulated them into it.

I didn't want to be like my mother.

"We have to go find him." I shifted again and tried to sit up but Olly put his arm out to stop me. "Please. We have to."

"I know, but we don't know where he is exactly and you need to heal."

"Heal me then," I said, grabbing his hand and putting it on my chest. "Heal me now."

The motivation was there. The command was

there. His eyes softened and he brought my hand to his lips and kissed my knuckles.

"She used some kind of demon bone knife. I can't heal the wound. Rafael can't either. You lost a lot of blood. They had to give you a transfusion of angel blood. That seemed to stop whatever autoimmune response you were having too because your temperature is back to normal."

I hadn't even been aware it was abnormal since it spiked to crazy high levels. How long ago was that? What day was it?

"Does the creator, or God, or whatever he's called, sound a bit like Morgan Freeman?" I wasn't going to say anything about my dream, but it was out of my mouth before I could stop myself.

Asher snorted and I looked at him. A smile crossed his face. "He sounds like whatever you want him to sound like."

"It felt so real. I-"

A loud rumble came from outside and the ground started to shake, the bed and machines moving. Olly and Tobias jumped up and rushed to the window with Asher.

"What is it?" I gripped the sheets and the shaking subsided fairly quickly.

The three angels stood at the window, staring out. A loud siren started blaring in the distance. At first it sounded like someone was lying on a car horn but then the sound became familiar. A sound that I had only heard in movies.

"An air raid?" Maybe this was another part of the dream I was having.

"Is that a motherfucking *dragon*?" Asher backed away from the window. "Holy shit, it's a fucking dragon. Dragons are real?"

My heart stopped. "It's a hell serpent. She said she wouldn't use it. I have to stop it!"

I didn't know how I'd stop it, but if I could command it to stop, maybe it would.

Tobias turned and he and Asher made their way to me, stopping me from getting out of the bed and yanking off all the wires and tubes.

"Uhh, guys!" Olly was still looking out the window. "It's headed this way."

The hospital room door slammed open and a man with quite the head of long blond hair pulled into a braid rushed in. He had a sword at his hip and looked all business. His eyes landed on me then went to Olly.

"Michael, what's-" Tobias started.

"Get her back to the academy. She'll be safe there." He was looking directly at Olly. "Do you understand, boy?"

"Yes, sir."

"She can't die. Not yet." With that, he turned and left as quickly as he'd appeared.

Not yet? What the actual fuck did that mean? I didn't have much time to think on it because my machines started beeping as things were unhooked. Olly scooped me into his arms and I winced.

Was the hell serpent coming for me? I shuddered as we entered the hall where there was a flurry of activity with doctors, nurses, and patients rushing around. The building shook again and I flinched as a plastic light cover fell from the ceiling in front of us.

I'd like to think I could have stopped the creature with a command, but who was I kidding? The only experience I had was practicing on John and commanding the two human security guards. A bus-sized hell serpent was something else entirely.

Asher, who was somehow keeping his shit together, opened the stairwell door and we followed Tobias up the stairs to the roof. It was for helicopters, but tonight it would be our launching pad.

A screech filled the night sky along with all of the sounds you'd expect when a giant, dragon-like creature was ravaging a city.

We had to be over thirty stories high. I clung to Olly's shirt. His wings came out just as the head of the serpent came into view. It was either smart as fuck or somehow was tracking us.

We took off from the roof just as it let out a screech and fire poured from its mouth. The entire top of the building went up in flames.

I knew this was just the beginning.

TO BE CONTINUED...

Coming in December! *Transcend* (Celestial Academy Book 3)
Available for preorder
https://books2read.com/u/3np96P

Coming in December! *Transcend*, Celestial Academy
Book 3
Available for preorder
https://books2read.com/u/3np96P

Be sure to join my Facebook group or signup for my
newsletter for book release updates and sneak
peaks!
https://www.facebook.com/
groups/mayanicoleauthor/

Newsletter
https://mailchi.mp/2441120a2b47/mayanicole

Instagram @mayanicoleauthor

Twitter @MayaAuthor